Culture Is Like Water

Sun Jiazheng

Foreign Languages Press

First Edition 2006

ISBN 7-119-04494-X
© Foreign Languages Press, Beijing, China, 2006
Published by Foreign Languages Press
24 Baiwanzhuang Road, Beijing 100037, China
Website: http: //www.flp.com.cn
Email Address: Info@flp.com.cn
Sales@flp.com.cn
Distributed by China International Book Trading Corporation
35 Chegongzhuang Xilu, Beijing 100044, China
P. O. Box 399, Beijing, China

Printed in the People's Republic of China

CONTENTS

Preface   i

I.
Adhering to the people-based, scientific development outlook and striving to build a harmonious society.   1

II.
In culture, China pursues a state of "harmony without uniformity."   15

III.
In cultural construction, the basic level is the root, and the people are the foundation.   39

IV.

Culture is like water, which silently seeps into and nurtures all forms of life.　55

V.

Mother culture is our root, and the foundation for creating new culture.　69

VI.

Chinese cultural tradition contains a kind of ideological vigor and spirit of innovation that ceaselessly reproduces and renews itself.　95

VII.

The Chinese cultural market is one with tremendous potential.　113

The influence of culture on society is extensive and profound. Speaking about the influence of the novel *Uncle Tom's Cabin* on the American Civil War, Abraham Lincoln said to its author Harriet Beecher-Stowe, "So you're the little woman who wrote the book that made this great war."

Culture is a field with a great variety of categories, different levels, functions and tolerance. Generally speaking, the functions and roles of culture in education, inspiration, molding of character, esthetics and enjoyment, are largely manifested in an indirect and profound way, and in subtle imperceptible change. In this sense, culture is like water, which silently seeps into and nurtures all forms of life.

Culture is the best channel to reach people's hearts. It does so gradually and once it enters the heart, its effects are far-reaching; in this sense, we can say that culture is like water that permeates into people's hearts.

The metaphor of using water for people has since long been a tradition in Chinese culture. Water has the virtue of benefiting all things on earth, the capacity to absorb hundreds of streams, the wisdom to give guidance in light of the general trend flex according to circumstances, the courage to continue a cause despite repeated setbacks, the beauty of the shapes given at the sight of things and the strength of constant dripping wearing away a stone.

Water symbolizes the harmonious spirit of today's China. I am reminded of a famous remark full of Oriental wisdom, the well-known quotation from Lao Zi, a great thinker of more than 2,000 years ago — "All that is best is like water."

Tremendous change has taken place in China since 1978. The greatest change is in people's inner world and the Chinese understanding of themselves and the world, which is the greatest and deepest change. The Chinese are building a new life, brimful of confidence, and closely linking their destiny with that of all mankind. They ardently love their country, and this world as well.

China has registered tremendous achievements in its reform and opening up to the outside world and the modernization drive. The profound changes that have taken place in China's economy, politics, culture and social life have attracted world attention. This ancient civilized country in the East, like a lively youngster, stands before the world. Many people in the world have noticed China's development and are casting their gaze in this direction. Culture is an important avenue for getting to know China, because culture is a direct reflection of the life and spiritual condition of a country and its people.

Since the start of reform and opening up in 1978, the Chinese have focused their attention on national development and improvement in people's livelihoods. So

China faces the world with an open-minded attitude, eager to learn from the rest of the world. As China advances toward the future, it still regards this learning from the world as having no finite end. Exchange between countries, like exchange between people, requires a teller and a listener, and sometimes it is more important to listen. When introducing Chinese culture to the world, it is we who are "telling," but we also want to become better at "listening" through the process of "telling," so that we can achieve deep-level communication between the peoples of China and all the world, with mutual knowledge and fellow feeling.

Culture reflects people's living, their feelings and ambitions. Conversely, it also exerts an active influence on people's existence and development, and, in this sense, culture also means people. Therefore, understanding today's Chinese culture means having a better knowledge and understanding of Chinese people of today.

Since the start of reform and opening up, China has witnessed enormous changes. That said, we are profoundly aware that China is still lagging far behind the world's developed countries. Furthermore, this change is not just about the high-rise buildings sprouting up everywhere, nor about the highways stretching out in every direction, still less the bald statistics; the greatest change is in how the Chinese people view themselves and the rest of the world. The change in the Chinese people's inner world is the greatest and most profound change. The Chinese people of today, particularly the younger ones, have come to realize that their own fate is inevitably closely tied to that of all humanity; they understand that while ardently loving their own country they should have the same love for the world; they face the world with a broad mind, eager as never before to join hands with the world in creating a better future for mankind.

While it is concerned with material development, China is showing ever-greater concern with development of mankind itself. Without concern for the humanities, without man's all-round development, and without harmony between men, or between man and nature, all development will lose its meaning. When foreign friends come to China, I always suggest that besides looking at the external changes, they should try as far as possible to contact and chat with ordinary Chinese, so as to get to know their lives and feelings, thereby gradually coming to know the inner world of the Chinese people.

I.

Adhering to the people-based, scientific development outlook and striving to build a harmonious society.

Firmly adhering to the people-based, scientific development outlook and striving to build a harmonious society not only act directly upon China's reform and opening up and socialist modernization; they become "internalized" as the cultural mindset of all society and "externalized" as the driving force propelling peaceful development in the world which is a mainstream ideal and value orientation in modern Chinese society.

At present, Chinese society is implementing the people-based, scientific development outlook, and striving to build a socialist harmonious society. This is extension and enhancement of the process of reform, opening up and development undertaken for more than two decades by Chinese society, and is the basic trend of Chinese social development. It is not only the national development strategy set down by the Chinese government, but is also a kind of mainstream cultural ideal and value orientation of Chinese society. Contemporary Chinese culture reflects the mental outlook of Chinese people of today and is an embodiment of their inner feelings and desires. Harmonious political views and social ideals deeply influence the rhythm of modern China's development, and influence the cultural refinement and spiritual richness of the Chinese people. In my view, taking this perspective on contemporary Chinese culture and the Chinese people living within it enables one to grasp from a di-

Chinese New Year picture

verse and complex situation the main "blood vessels" of Chinese culture, and to grasp the main spirit of the Chinese today from the rich and varied expressions of such spirit.

Adhering to the people-based, scientific development outlook, advocating the human spirit summed up in the phrase "peace is most precious" is an expression of typically Chinese feeling. This being the case, it deeply stirred the hearts of Chinese people as soon as it was proposed, and gave rise to widespread favorable comments in the world at large. Harmonious cultural spirit grows out of the cultural soil of the Chinese people. In China, advocating harmony is a long cultural tradition. Beginning over 2,200 years ago in the pre-Qin period, "peace" has been one of our most important philo-

CULTURE IS LIKE WATER

The Forbidden City — the world's largest extant imperial palace

sophical concepts. From one generation to the next, related theories were contributed in an unending thread. The balance of *yin* and *yang*, and the complementarity of hardness and softness were looked upon as the true law of the universe; harmony in human relations and coordination in society were seen as the perfect social relationship; assimilation with heaven and earth, and peaceful coexistence with all things were regarded as the perfect state of existence. In the history of ideas in China, the philosophy and esthetic ideal in almost every school of thought regarded harmony as a basic theme and value; China's multifarious folk cultures are overflowing with harmonious spirit ... "holding to the center without being extreme," "taking delight in peace and getting closer to benevolence," "chiming in with peace and making harmony possible."

Upholding harmony expresses Oriental wisdom's insight into life and everything in the cosmos. Human society has all along been faced with three basic contradictions: contradiction between man and nature, the internal contradiction of human society, and personal contradiction. Transforming contradiction into harmony has always been the dream and pursuit of China and humankind. In 2005, I accompanied M. Jean-Pierre Raffarin, former French Prime Minister, to Beijing's Palace Museum, the largest imperial palace in the world, during which visit I talked with him about China's traditional culture. I told him that the names of the three halls of the Imperial Palace's key buildings are a concentrated reflection of Chinese traditional philosophical ideas. The Hall of Supreme Harmony — the auspicious sign of heaven and earth — is a metaphor for harmony between man and nature; the Hall of Complete Harmony — the golden mean and mildness — is a metaphor for the harmony between man and the world; the Hall of Preserving Harmony — a peaceful mind and good health — is a metaphor for harmony between mind the body. The names of the three halls reflect the value ori-

Culture is like water

entation of China's traditional culture, that is, the pursuit of harmony. That said, independence of the country, liberation of the nation and freedom of the people are prerequisites for social harmony; for these things the Chinese people have fought indomitably in a protracted struggle. Harmony is something that has been avidly sought by the Chinese people for thousands of years and is an essential feature of Chinese culture. In certain historical contexts this may express itself as resistance and struggle; furthermore, in the process of building a harmonious society, there will still be contradiction within harmony and the cutting edge in the most melodious verse, but the goal is to find final harmony. It can be said that the Chinese people's aspiration for a harmonious life has never changed.

The harmonious spirit advocated today not only contains the cream of tradition but is also endowed with the connotations of our times. President Hu Jintao has expounded the six-faceted contents of and basic requirements for the building of a harmonious society, namely: democracy and rule of law; fairness and justice; creditability and friendship; fullness of vigor, stability and orderliness, and harmonious coexistence between man and nature. To put these into practice, we show greater concern than ever before about people's values, rights and interests, freedom, quality of life, development potential and happiness index. We also pay more attention to the coordinated development of economy, politics, culture and society, to the harmonious coexistence between man and nature. The Chinese people are now engaged in the building of a well-off society in an all-round way and working hard to open up a new phase in the endeavor to build socialism with Chinese characteristics. Thanks to these efforts, the reform and opening up program has entered a crucial historical period. This is "a period of development opportunity," as well as "a period of striking contradictions." Only when we uphold the scientific development outlook and take construction of a harmonious society as the goal set for making progress, can we adapt ourselves to the profound changes in China's social structure and social life, lead Chinese society onto the road of sustainable development and create a happy life for the Chinese people.

In the past 28 years since China launched the reform and opening up policy, the country has made monumental achievements in the modernization drive, basically bringing about a relatively comfortable life for the people. Between 1978 and 2005, China's gross domestic product (GDP) went up from US$147.3 billion to US$2225.7 billion, an average annual growth of 9.5 percent. The maintenance of a strong momentum for the sustained growth of China's economy, the continuous enhancement of comprehensive national strength and unbroken improvement in people's livelihood represent really extraordinary progress. Failure to notice this progress, exaggeration and overplaying the problems that do exist here is not in accordance with reality; but neither is it in line with reality to overestimate China's development and current state, to regard China as a developed country already. Although China has recorded historic progress, the Chinese leadership is quite sober-minded about it. China is a developing country with a population of over 1.3 billion and quite a weak foundation to start with. Take GDP for example. Although China's GDP has entered the front ranks in the world, its per-capita GDP is not even in the first 100 among the world's 200-plus countries. China's regions differ vastly from one another; many people live in rural areas and their living standards are lagging behind that of urban dwellers. China's poor rural population has decreased from 250 million five years ago to the present 23.65 million, and these people live on less than half a US dollar per day per capita. Their living conditions

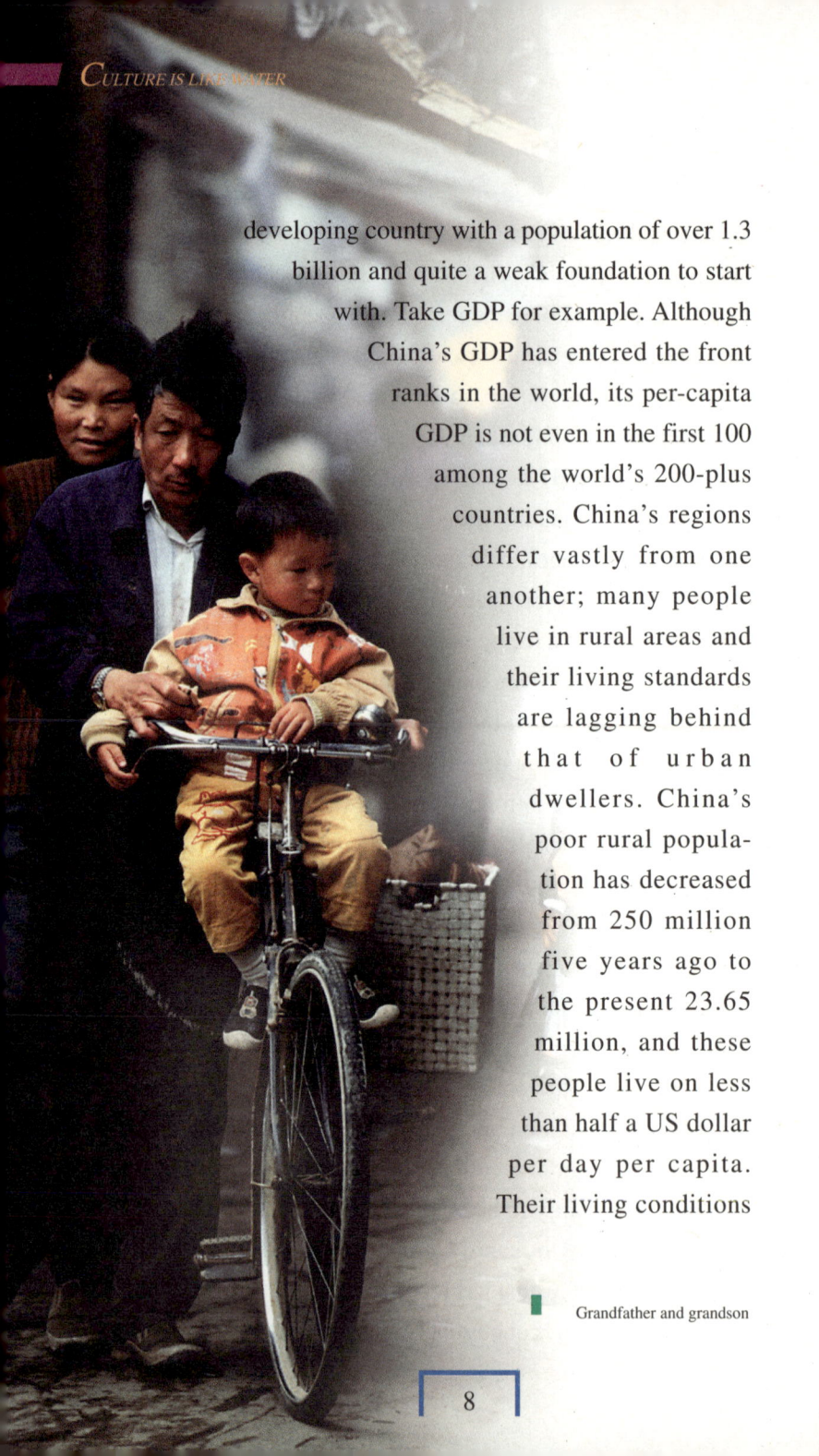

▪ Grandfather and grandson

are still a great concern for us. In October 2005, I paid a visit to the United States, during which I discovered that many Americans overestimated China's development and harbored hidden worries. I told them my view, "Now, when people are just feeling a touch of autumn cool, the Chinese government has already been thinking about how to enable farmers living in poverty-stricken regions to pass the winter with adequate food and clothing. China's circumstances determine that the country has to go through long-term hardship and struggle in order to completely realize modernization. After

A woman carrying a basket on her back, ancient Phoenix City, Hunan

28 years of effort, we have basically solved the problem of feeding the Chinese people, supporting 23 percent of the world's population with only seven percent of the world's arable land, and we have basically brought about a relatively affluent life for the Chinese people. However, as a philosopher once said, "When people are hungry, they have only one worry, but once their bellies are full, countless worries come up within them." The former concern is survival; the latter concern is worries about development. It is precisely through the process of constantly solving problems in development that Chinese society is gradually advancing towards an ideal state. "Engaging in construction with concentrated attention, and seeking development with one heart and one mind" is a slogan long etched deep into the heart of Chinese society. Successive Chinese governments have devoted their utmost energy to solving domestic problems, such as the livelihood of 1.3 billion people. When its 1.3 billion people live and work in contentment, leading a prosperous life, when China is developed and harmonious, then its strength to promote world peace and development would be enhanced. Such an achievement could be described as China's greatest contribution to the world. China has many problems left over from history and will encounter lots of problems in the course of development; it will take the efforts of several generations to solve these problems and construct an ideal, harmonious society. But since we understand the loftiness of our goal, we will not fear the long road we have to take in order to reach it.

The requirement to build a harmonious society is consistently manifested in every field of work of the Chinese government and Chinese people, and has become a kind of governing direction and standard for society, a kind of spiritual ethos directing social practice. Therefore, it not only acts directly upon reform and opening-up and the socialist modernization drive; it goes further, becoming "internalized" into the cultural mindset of society as a whole, nurturing the spiritual world of the Chinese people, exerting its influence in stealthy and invisible fashion, like the life-giving force of spring, deeply affecting the life and temperament of every member of society and on the collective consciousness of our people, becoming a kind of cultural spirit that can govern social thinking and social conduct.

The ideal of building a harmonious society is making a profound "external transformation" into a driving force by which the Chinese people resolutely follow the road of peaceful development. The pursuit of harmony actually has always deeply influenced New China's foreign relations. It is the ideological foundation on which the Chinese government has long upheld the Five Principles of Peaceful Coexistence, and is the source of strength for the Chinese people to advance world peaceful development. In their harmony-oriented social value system, the Chinese people, as a force in the construction of a harmonious world, have become more conscious and resolute in their determination to carry forward this mission.

The Chinese ancients always compared themselves to

CULTURE IS LIKE WATER

all things in the world, believing that there were fundamental points of sameness and of correspondence between them, believing in the oneness of man and nature, and that all things on earth were governed by the same law. Moreover, man's conduct always began with the self, and then was extended towards other people and things. The concepts that "a gentleman relies first on himself and then on others" and "providing for my aged parents first and then extending the same to the aged of others, taking care of my own children first and extend the same to the children of others," both expressed the idea of treating others as you would treat yourself.

This logic of understanding and conduct acts deeply upon the Chinese of today, so that in the process of building a harmonious

■ Multi-part singing of Dong people

society, China pays special attention to individual development and self-perfection, to a person's inner peace, to harmony between man and society, and between man and nature. This is an omni-dimensional and universal pursuit and is deeply ingrained into the Chinese people's way of life and social condition. When all citizens take harmony as their purpose, the pursuit of world harmony will be not just the resolve and actions of the government, but of all citizens, thus providing a deeper, broader and more solid cultural foundation for the government's foreign policy of peaceful development. Hence, the Chinese government's efforts for world peace have been incorporated into the grand backdrop and larger context of harmonious coexistence between the Chinese people and all things on earth. It is precisely because the Chinese genuinely regard harmony as what they want for their own character, and the inner structure of a harmonious society as their own firm and unshakable goal, that China's purpose of safeguarding world peace and promoting common development, and its aspirations for achieving a harmonious world have become even more resolute and more sincere.

The building of a harmonious society now underway across our vast land and our efforts beyond China to build a harmonious world together with the world's peoples both involve the existence of corresponding relations and structures. As we energetically go about building a harmonious society, China will not only realize harmonious economic and social development within China; beyond our borders we will also give stronger prominence to the theme of peaceful development, and more clearly display to the world China's inherent ethos of harmony. China believes that its harmonious spirit and that same spirit in the cultures of other nations of the world will re-echo and merge together giving a common expression to a kind of universal human truth. From the basis of this globally recognized philosophy and predicated culture, we shall work to realize mutual caring between different groups, mutual tolerance between different civilizations, and peaceful coexistence among different nations, promoting the gradual realization of a harmonious world.

II.

In culture, China pursues a state of "harmony without uniformity."

In culture, China implements the domestic policy of "letting a hundred flowers blossom and letting a hundred schools of thought contend." Internationally it advocates maintaining the diversity of world culture, and pursues a state of "harmony without uniformity." Every country has the right to choose its own culture: like a fish chooses water and a bird opts for the forest, they know what they need.

In today's world, peaceful development is the mainstream course, but destabilizing factors do still exist that impact on peaceful development. For some time now, many shocking incidents have been taking place in the world. Social development imbalance, the widening gap between and rich and poor, the worsening eco-environment, terrorism running riot and unbridled cross-border crimes — such factors, when woven together, constitute a threat to the survival of our species. Where is the human race heading? Which way will the world develop? In the future world, what laws should we follow? These questions loom before the world's people more gravely than ever before.

On the domestic front, the Chinese government is to build a harmonious society, seeking peace, prosperity and happiness for all the Chinese people; in foreign affairs, it is bound to the unwavering pursuit of an independent foreign policy of peace, wishing for friendly coexistence with vari-

Confucius, ancient China's great thinker and teacher

ous other countries, seeking peace, cooperation and common development and jointly building a harmonious world. In the process of building a harmonious society, the vision and the minds of the Chinese are expanded; for the Chinese people there is a close association between their own tranquility and happiness and world peace and development.

The pursuit of harmony and the aspiration for peace originate from the profound tradition of the Chinese people, come out of the fundamental interests of the country and represent the Chinese people's profound lesson learned from bitter experience in the modern age. After the 1840s, China became poorer and weaker, and for more than one hundred years it suffered incessant foreign aggression; the Chinese people rose in resistance when faced with the danger of national subjugation and racial extinction, finally winning independence and liberation. More than 2,000 years ago, the thinker Confucius said, "Do not do to others what you would not have them do to you," and this is the moral standard to which the Chinese adhere, as well as the golden rule for handling relations between countries. The Chinese people, who have undergone enormous suffering from menace and aggression in the past, more than ever cherish their hard-won peace. The Chinese people are well aware that China's security and interests are closely related to world security and interests. As "a bird sings to draw a friend's response," the Chinese people will at all times and in all places corroborate the peace-loving intentions of the people of all nations in the world.

For a period of time, the residual dregs of the so-called "China threat" have been resurfacing. It is impossible for us to change the viewpoints of the minority who hold this view, because prejudice is even more immune to facts and truth than ignorance is. For most people, any doubts and worries they have stem from the fact that they do not really know the actual situation in China, nor do they understand China's cultural tradition. I remember that at the 30th anniversary of the normalization of Sino-Japanese diplomatic relations, I delivered a speech in Tokyo in which I stressed that China's development represents an opportunity for rather than a threat to Japan or the world at large. If one approaches the issue by looking at history and reality together, then it will be clear to all fair-minded people that the so-called "China threat" just does not stand up.

Firstly, in its history China has suffered a great deal from "threats" and aggression. After the 1840s, China was made ever poorer, ever weaker for over a century, during which period almost every Western power committed aggression against China. The country and its people were virtually wiped out. The Chinese people had to wage continuous struggle to save the country and ensure its survival.

Secondly, the theory of the "China threat" does not conform to China's reality and national policy. Some foreigners have asked me: Using the simplest terms, how would you sum up modern China? I think China's current status and development trend can be accurately summed up in three words, the first of which is "reform" — reform and opening up being tied together. For more than 20 years, China's reform and opening up program has kept on advancing; China faces the world with a more open mind, learning from the world's advanced science, culture and technology, and only by so doing can our ancient nation maintain its vitality. The second word is "development." In the late 1970s, China entered the new historical period of reform and opening up. What is the greatest change China has made over the past 20-plus years? It is that we discarded the slogan "class struggle as the key link." Instead, we took economic development and improvement of people's livelihoods as the central task of the country. China is the largest developing country, it is an onerous and long-term task to develop economy and culture and improve people's livelihoods. The Chinese people keep firmly in their minds Deng Xiaoping's instruction "development is the absolute principle." The development we refer to here is coordinated development of politics, economy and culture, harmonious development between man and society and between man and nature. This is the Chinese government's long-term, enduring principle. The third word is "stability." China boasts 56 ethnic groups and a population of over 1.26 billion; without stability, nothing can be achieved. The crucial factors behind the phenomenal achievements that China has made in the short space of 20-odd years are unity among various ethnic groups, social stability and progress. "Reform, development and stability" can best sum up today's China and can best reflect China's current domestic policy. China's principle in foreign relations is an extension of the principle that guides its internal affairs. "Safeguarding world peace and promoting common development" is the Chinese government's unshakable purpose, as well as the desire and determination of all the Chinese people. The Chinese government has repeatedly emphasized that China will not seek hegemony and will not threaten others even if it becomes strong.

Thirdly, the theory of the "China threat" contradicts the trends of our times. To see the development of another country as a threat to oneself originates essentially from a Cold War mentality. After the disintegration of the bipolar world pattern, the trends of our times have been economic globalization, political multi-polarization and cultural diversification. Emerging from the shadow of the Cold War, more and more people have come to realize that men's fates are interconnected. How does China handle inter-state relations? This can be summed up as follows: In politics, mutual trust to seek security; in economic affairs, mutual benefit and win-win results in pursuit of development; and in culture, mutual respect, equality and exchange to seek prosperity. China's stance and attitude are widely approved and supported. It can be said that this represents the trends of our times and feelings of the people. At the time of the Asian financial crisis in 1997, the Chinese economy was also under tremendous pressure. At the time, there was discussion in domestic academic circles about whether the Renminbi (RMB) should be devalued. But the Chinese government was of the opinion that whilst RMB devaluation would, of course, alleviate pressure on China, it was bound to impact on some Asian countries and that China, as a member of the large world family, should not shift the burden onto others at this difficult time. China acted as a responsible country, resolutely not devaluing the RMB. Currently, the Chinese government is striving to scientifically adjust the RMB exchange rate mechanism under the condition of establishing a market economy.

Culture is like water

The Temple of Heaven

Culture is like water

Fourthly, the theory of the "China threat" contradicts the present state and goal of the development of Sino-Japanese relations. China and Japan are important countries, both in Asia and the whole world. Geographically close and culturally linked, our two countries are highly complementary. The period of the last 20 years or so has seen China's fastest ever economic development; for Japanese enterprises it has been the period of greatest benefit from cooperation with China. China is a developing country while Japan is a developed country; there is still a clear gap between the two countries in terms of science-technology level, business management and economic development stage. Japan's gross national product (GNP) is US$5 trillion, while China's is US$1 trillion; in terms of per-capita GNP the gap between the two is even more obvious. The respective economic development stages and situations of China and Japan are different; the economies of the two countries are highly complementary and one can say that cooperation between us is greater than competition between us. China's development can bring only opportunities to Japan. Economic development requires the support of a kind of advanced cultural idea. The 21st century will be a century of culture; and one important factor determining whether or not economic development that has reached a certain stage can advance to a new level is its cultural idea; speaking from a broader perspective, it depends upon the cultural quality of a people. If China and Japan are to expand and strengthen their economic cooperation, cultural links seem more important than ever before

Several years have passed, and although relations between our two countries have experienced new twists and turns, the basic viewpoint of the Chinese has not changed in any respect. What is more, China is building a harmonious society at home and on the international front is joining its efforts with the people of various countries to build a harmonious world; in my opinion, this fact will mean even fewer buyers for the theory of the "China threat."

As regards cultural development, China pursues the principle of "letting a hundred flowers blossom and a hundred schools of thought contend" at home; outside China it supports the diversity of world culture. Each country has the right to choose its own culture; they and only they have the say whether a certain kind of culture fits them, like fish choose water and birds opt for the forest, they know what they need. No matter how others evaluate our ideological and institutional cultures, it is we ourselves who are clearest about whether "the shoe fits." Cultural divergence between different peoples is an objective reality that comes with history, and an essential prerequisite if the world is to maintain its rich and colorful variety. The thinking and attitudes adopted towards these differences will lead to two diametrically opposed consequences. On the one hand, advocating "harmony without uniformity" and promoting better understanding and tolerance to realize mutual beneficial results and advance to peaceful coexistence. On the other, persisting in the obso-

CULTURE IS LIKE WATER

lete Cold War mentality, spreading suspicion, envy and estrangement, thus triggering friction, confrontation and even war. Humanity should take its own destiny into its own hands. It is gratifying that the world is increasingly of one mind about this. Adherence to the national character of cultures, inheriting and carrying forward the best cultural traditions of various peoples are prerequisites for cultural diversity. The cultures of different peoples cannot replace one another; if cultures have no national character, there can be no cultural diversity. The more a culture belongs to its people, the more it belongs to the world. The world's various peoples all have their unique cultures and traditions; in the process of their development, they draw on and adopt from each other extensively, fusing into new forms, but must retain their distinct and independent character. The cultural tradition of each people, as their unique spiritual wealth, is an important source of cultural creative strength and the foundation for world cultural development. Increasing modernization has brought

■ Wonderful performance given by international artistes

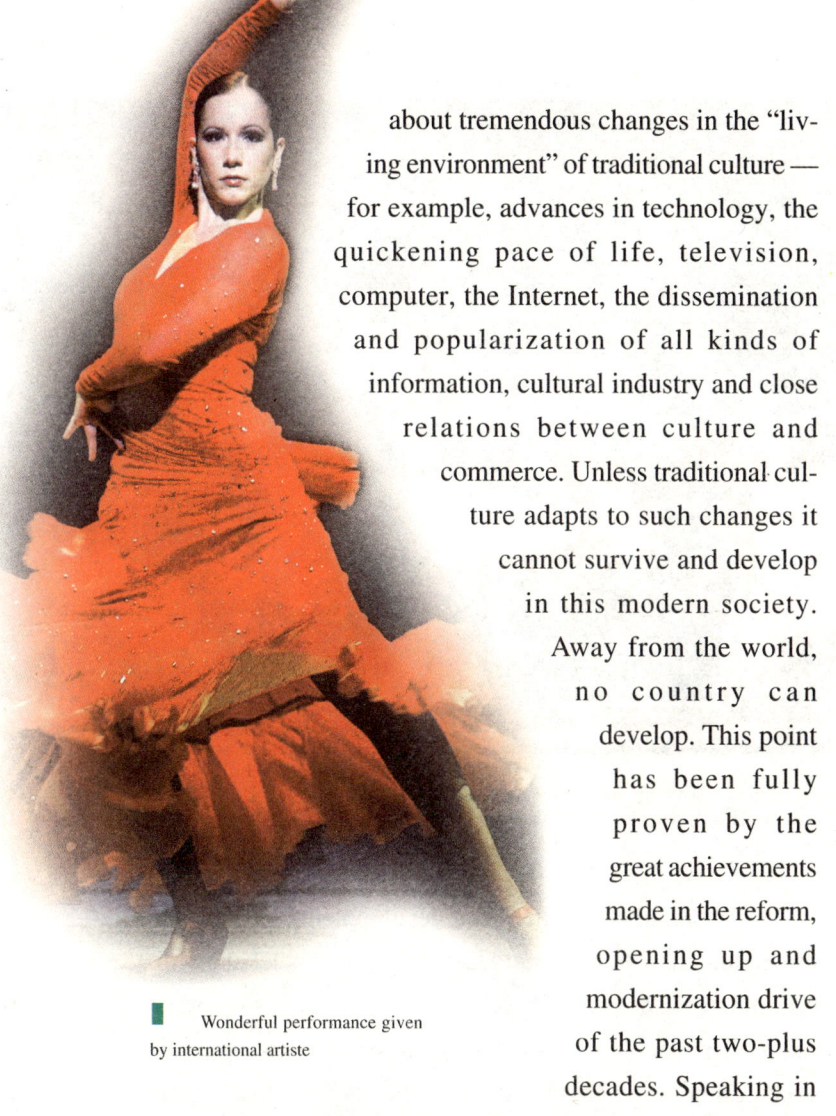

about tremendous changes in the "living environment" of traditional culture — for example, advances in technology, the quickening pace of life, television, computer, the Internet, the dissemination and popularization of all kinds of information, cultural industry and close relations between culture and commerce. Unless traditional culture adapts to such changes it cannot survive and develop in this modern society. Away from the world, no country can develop. This point has been fully proven by the great achievements made in the reform, opening up and modernization drive of the past two-plus decades. Speaking in terms of culture itself, it is precisely the exchange, stimulation, drawing from and fusion among different cultures that constitute the indispensable condition for stimulating creative power and enhancing vitality.

The cultures of various peoples around the world have

Wonderful performance given by international artiste

Wonderful performance given by international artistes

different traditions and their own development roads; different traditional cultures should learn from each other and seek common prosperity, not excluding the cultures of other peoples. There are very obvious differences between traditional Chinese and Western cultures. For example: as regards cognitive approach, the West values rationalism and reasoning while China stresses experience and intuition; the West puts the emphasis on microscopic detailed analysis, whilst China emphasizes the macrocosmic integral whole. In the judgment of values, the Chinese usually keep their eyes on the long range whilst Westerners, Americans in particular, are more "here and now." In interpersonal relations, the West emphasizes competition, usefulness and ability, China gives attention to social ethics, morality and spirit. As regards self-appraisal, the West stresses the individual and self promotion; China, on the other hand, has always paid attention to "cultivating self-morality" and "self-examination." Exchange between different cultures not only makes it possible to know the other side, but also helps one understand oneself. A historical comparison of Western and Chinese cultures reveals that there are many interesting things we can learn from each other. Given human progress and the trends of our age, no civilization can develop on its own or survive in isolation; exchange, learning from each other's experiences and mutual complementarity between Eastern and Western civilizations and other countries' cultures are in line with the trends of our age and how people feel. Contact between different cultural traditions helps to dispel estrangement and prejudice between peoples and is conducive to developing political and economic relations between countries. It also facilitates the common development of culture predicated on the preservation of cultural diversity.

A famous American TV anchorman once asked me, "Is the 21st century China's century?" I clearly expressed my disagreement. The earth is the common homeland of humankind and the 21st century is the century which we all share.

Countries, big or small, rich or poor, are all equal. Only when men live in peaceful coexistence and join their hands together, can they have a beautiful future. Diversity of culture, like the diversity of living things, is not a proposition, but an objective reality. The Chinese government initiated and held the first ASEM Asia-Europe Conference on Cultures and Civilizations in Beijing in 2003; the first Asian Forum of Culture Ministers and the 7th Asian Art Festival were successfully held in Foshan, Guangdong Province in 2005; the second ministerial conference of the Sino-Arab Forum and the Arab World Art Festival were held in China in 2006. These forums and activities transcended the unified globalization pattern, embodied the spirit of mutual respect, responding to the diversity and complexity of the world situation. Ministers at these forums arrived at this consensus: Diversity of culture is a basic characteristic of world culture, and an expression of world civilization. As cultural policy makers, our minds should be broader and larger, should have a brand-new historical view, really proceed from the development needs of world culture and civilization, develop cultural exchange among various countries on an equal footing, and jointly create a new structure for human cultures in all their richness and diversity.

Forming mechanisms for cultural exchange and development between various countries, strengthening relations and dialogue and reducing conflicts and frictions help achieve the successful passing on and development of traditional culture within the process of economic globalization. Cultural development requires the creation of an environment for mutual exchange between various peoples. Hence, respecting, learning from and exchanging between cultures and forming a set of basic principles and effective mechanisms for cultural contact will become a common issue facing various countries. These principles and mechanisms should not only cover the overwhelming majority of countries, but also should, to a certain degree, be workable. In a speech I made last year in the United States, I said that China and the United States are separated by a vast ocean and have completely different historical backgrounds; but we each have vast territories, and both are countries where different ethnic groups live side by side, where a variety of cultures mix and whose peoples are hardworking and smart. China and the United States differ vastly from each other and this difference naturally may bring with it certain collisions and frictions. But at the same time, it is precisely this difference that produces a mutual attraction. Without this difference, the world might be a quieter place, but a considerably duller and more dreary one. In my opinion, while acknowledging the diversity of the world, we also need to see the similarities present within that diversity. Diversity makes contact essential between different cultures, and the existence of similarities makes that contact possible. Of our two countries China is the largest developing country in the world and the United States is the biggest developed country in the

Culture is like water

Bustling street scenes in France during the China-France Culture Year held at the start of the new millennium

world; the peoples of our two countries are kind-hearted and creative. They each have a vast market, and economically they are strongly complementary. In many spheres our countries share common national interests — especially in anti-terrorism, in the safeguarding of global and regional security, in the protection of the international environment and other

Culture is like water

global issues, in economy and trade, scientific and technological and cultural exchange. They can draw on and learn from each other's experiences in many respects. Some people are prone to exaggerate the differences and frictions between China and the United States and between their cultures, and ignore our common interests and compatibility. It is normal to have differences, and conflicts should be no cause for surprise; what is crucial is for mutual respect, consulting with each other on the basis of equality, and tackling contradictions and problems with a frank and sincere attitude and on the principle of mutual benefit and reciprocity. Ascending a height to get perspective on something is the Chinese way of thinking; attention to detail is the American pragmatic spirit. A combination of the two approaches help us to a clear view of popular feeling and the general trend, and is of help when discussing and tackling specific problems. Only through dialogue is it possible to test each other, complement each other and act upon each other to attain common development. This is true of bilateral relations between China and the United States; other bilateral and multilateral relations are basically the same too. Contacts should be further strengthened between different countries, peoples and cultures, discovering in the process of linkage how different cultures achieve the same goal by different means, and the beauty of communication and accord.

Merging into the international community with a more open attitude and further expanding cultural exchange with foreign countries is the firm and unshakable cultural policy of China. Modern cultural construction is going on against the larger backdrop of modern information technology and economic globalization. Given human progress and the trends of our age, no civilization can develop on its own or survive in isolation; it can be said that the long-term coexistence and mutual exchange between Eastern and Western civilizations and the cultures of various countries are in line with mainstream trends and with popular feelings. The development of Chinese culture cannot be achieved without the common development of human civilization. Opening to the outside world not only is a basic national policy for China's economic construction, but also is one of the fundamental guidelines for China's modern cultural construction. Under the guidance of this policy, China's modern cultural construction has fully demonstrated its openness, being oriented toward modernization, toward the world and toward the future. To date, China has signed agreements on cultural cooperation with more than 100 countries and signed over 400 plans for implementation of cultural exchanges; has established cultural contacts in different forms with over 160 countries and regions, and maintains various forms of links with thousands of foreign and international cultural organizations. The scope of cultural exchange with foreign countries covers many aspects such as literature, art, cultural relics, books, museums, news, publishing, broadcasting, movies, television, physical culture, education, science and technology, public health, youth, women, tourism and religion. Great quantities of famous foreign literary and social science works have been translated and introduced to China. Numerous excellent foreign works of art have been introduced to China. In recent years, we have concentrated our strength on holding a series of large-scale foreign cultural events, examples being the "China-France Year of Culture," the "Chinese Cultural Festival" in America, and "Chinese Culture's Journey to Africa." The "Year of Culture" has become China's national brand in its contacts with foreign countries. We have held the gala party titled "Get Together in Beijing," the Shanghai International Art Festival, Beijing International Music Festival, Wuqiao International Acrobatic Festival, Wuhan International Acrobatic Festival, vocal music, piano and violin international artistic contests and other international multilateral cultural activities, gathering together top artists and works of art from nearly one hundred countries, all warmly received by the Chinese people. At the same time as actively bringing in and adopting the strong points of others, we work hard to present our own national culture; the quality of the cultural and artistic programs dispatched is improving every day and Chinese artists have participated in music, dance, acrobatic and many other international arts competitions and festivals. All these demonstrate to the full the open stance of China's modern cultural construction and it is precisely this unprecedented openness that has given such an enormous boost to the development of the Chinese cultural industry and the prosperity of Chinese literature and art. Practice has proved that closing oneself from the outside indicates ossification and decline, whilst openness signifies vitality and development.

We are self-confident, therefore we greet with open hearts the cultural winds from every direction in the world; we are tenacious, therefore one can see in us shades of Xuanzang, the seventh-century Buddhist monk who journeyed to India to find the true scriptures and of Monk Ganjin (Jianzhen) who made seven trips to Japan to teach Buddhism. Opening to the outside world is China's basic national policy. Chinese culture, through the experience of reform and opening up, has been baptized and nourished in its meeting and mingling with world culture, and in turn the unique character and image of Chinese culture have added luster to world culture. Years of experience in cultural construction makes me see more clearly that Chinese culture is full of calls for concern for the humanities, which are always heard re-echoing along the "long corridor of world culture;" the awareness of worry and the sense of social responsibility inherent in Chinese culture can always be sure of a sympathetic response from persons of insight in other countries. The protection of China's cultural heritage actually is to hold fast to the common spiritual wealth of humankind; with each new cultural innovation in an unceasing process, China places its own starting point on the new horizon of world culture, sharing with the people of the world the best of its own cultural fruits; the Chinese cultural market does not live in isolation, it should have its own position and its own role in the world cultural market. Chinese culture is, after all, an organic component of world culture and is closely related to world cultural diversity. Particularly since China opened its door to the outside world, Chinese culture and world culture have become ever more inseparable, the healthy development of Chinese culture is inseparable from a rich world culture and harmonious environment.

III.

In cultural construction, the basic level is the root, and the people are the foundation.

In cultural construction, the basic level is the root, and the people are the foundation. Neither development nor happiness can be achieved by relying solely on material things; it is my hope that Chinese and foreign businessmen and entrepreneurs engaged in cultural undertakings will listen and respond to public calls for concern for the humanities to meet their cultural needs.

People are the mainstay in the building of a harmonious society, the starting point and the results of constructing a harmonious society; the essence and core of a harmonious society lie in all-round improvement of people's quality and full play to their initiative in various aspects. The harmonious society that China is to build is one that respects the interests and demands of various social groups, a society in which the masses of the people work according to their abilities and get their due, and in which the people enjoy an affluent life, peace and happiness. In terms of culture, it is to safeguard the basic cultural rights and interests of all citizens, satisfy the multi-layered and multi-faceted cultural demands of all society and to realize people's all-round development.

From start to last, human society has always developed and advanced amidst numerous and complex contradictions. It is a global issue as regards how to defuse various kinds of contradictions in the process of modernization and raise citizens' happiness index. Harmony is predicated on the contradiction and difference of things. Harmony means balance in movement, coordination in difference, orderliness in complexity and unity in diversity. Harmony is a concept in relativity and is developing. The people-based, scientific development outlook and the goal of building a socialist harmonious society represent the fundamental interests of the broadest section of the Chinese people, in tune with development trends in human society; it is also based on the reality of China's socialism being at the primary stage. This is a great journey, one bringing constant benefits to the broadest section of the Chinese people; it is also a tortuous road full of painful exploration and tenacious struggle. We will give full play to the role of culture in comforting and stimulating people's spirit, in diverting and alleviating social conflicts, and in bringing affinity and cohesion to members of society.

Proceeding from the consideration of putting people first, the Chinese government safeguards people's cultural rights and interests in the same way that it safeguards their political and economic rights and interests. The fundamental aim of cultural construction is satisfaction of people's daily growing cultural demands. To this end, we strive to find out the facts, pay attention to investigation and study, and endeavor to grasp how culture and citizens' cultural requirements are changing in our times. In our opinion, at present, this change is manifested mainly in the following:

One, total cultural demand shows considerable growth. Along with the rise in material living standards, the proportion of cultural spending to people's spending on daily necessities shows a continuous rise. Since the start of reform and opening-up, the Engel's coefficient for China's urban and rural households fell from 57.5 percent and 67.7 percent respectively in 1978 to 36.7 percent and 45.5 percent in 2005. There has been a corresponding rapid growth in cultural expenditure; urban and rural residents' per-capita spending on recreation, education and cultural services as a proportion of the daily life expenditure total is showing ballooning growth. This shows that once their material needs have been initially satisfied, people will pay more attention to their own

Chinese traditional dragon dance

all-round development and to a rich spiritual and cultural life; this is an expression of social progress. In the first two decades of the new millennium, the demands of cultural consumption will be stronger than before, the task of cultural construction will become heavier, and work in the cultural field can look forward to a bright future.

Two, society is more demanding about the quality of cultural products and cultural services. Along with economic development, higher living standards, greater awareness of developing themselves in an all-round way and building a new life, along with the faster and wider spread of culture that comes with technology advances, citizens' demands for better quality cultural products and services will become more pronounced. Only when cultural construction provides in-time excellent product and super-quality service in terms of information provision, knowledge support, enlightened thinking and esthetics, can it satisfy citizens' daily growing spiritual and cultural demands; only then can it give play to its unique and important role in promoting the steady release of productive force, people's all-round development and the all-round progress of society.

Three, cultural consumption will become more diversified and market-oriented. Along with the change in China's economic and social lives, people's production methods and lifestyles are becoming more varied, so their cultural requirements are also characterized by diversity, development and autonomous choice; the individual cultural demands of different ages, and different groups of people have become increasingly evident. This requires that the provision of our cultural products and services must be varied and rich, and that they develop and become perfected in the cultural market; only then can such changing, growing and multi-layered cultural demands be satisfied.

Four, the forms and methods of production, dissemination and consumption of cultural products are more scientific and modernized. The methods, ways and means by which people get their information, leisure and recreation are increasingly modern; some transmission media and cultural and recreational methods attract huge audiences and the influence of Internet technology on cultural life is becoming ever-greater.

Five, the degree of and demand for exchange between different cultures get deeper with each passing day. As the trends towards economic globalization and multi-polar politics continue to develop, international cultural exchange is continuously expanding. The interaction among different cultures will intensify with each passing day. The main orientation for cultural exchange with foreign countries for some time to come will be to maintain the independent character of Chinese culture and, in the process of safeguarding the distinct character of national culture, to safeguard the diversity and complementarity of world culture.

To this end, the Chinese government, centering on prosperity and development, is to improve the quality of life and

The Chinese government has vowed to build a learning society.

development capability of all members of society by means of excellent cultural products and services; culture will be a means to influence, inspire and comfort, to enhance people's sense of richness in their inner world, to create in them a sense of tranquil, happy spirit, thereby stimulating creativity. We should persist in emphasizing cultural construction, and devote a major effort to building a study-oriented society in which all people engage in study and in life-long study, set up a more complete cultural innovation system, a system of cultural laws, a public cultural service system and a cultural market system, and establish a cultural management system and operational mechanisms conducive to firing the enthusiasm of cultural workers, to producing more excellent products and to turning out more talents.

In cultural construction, the basic level is the root, and people are the foundation. Culture belongs to the people. The masses of the people not only enjoy culture, they also create culture. Culture has been said to "live among the people and die in temples;" it lives when it takes root among the masses and dies when it separates itself from the people. Only when the center of gravity of cultural work is located within people's real lives, only when the emphasis is on serving the grass roots, can it have the wide support of society, and maintain flesh-and-blood ties with the masses of

Beijing opera maintains close ties with the masses. Picture shows two grannies preparing for a performance.

Dragon-boat contest

the people.

While striving to meet the cultural demands of various social sectors, we should also pay special attention to safeguarding the cultural interests of the elderly, minors, migrant workers, the handicapped and other special groups.

The Chinese government has always paid great attention and consideration to the needs of the elderly, providing preferential services, earnestly satisfying their requirements in many areas, in material, spiritual and cultural life, in medical and health care, and protecting their rights and interests. Focusing on communities, neighborhoods, villages and towns, the government has, in recent years, increased its own funding, encouraged the entry of social funds and built cultural, health care and community services and other public facilities closely related to the daily life of the elderly. Cultural activities for the elderly are getting livelier day by day; quite a few places have established universities for the elderly, television universities and online schools for the elderly; cultural and sports organizations suited to the characteristics and needs of old people have been set up and scientific, healthy and civilized lifestyles are encouraged. The government also encourages seniors to continue participating in economic and social public welfare activities, regarding their knowledge and experience as precious social wealth.

The Chinese government has adopted a series of measures to strengthen cultural services for minors. It has opened wide the door of public-good cultural facilities to minors, strengthened the construction and management of cultural bases intended specially for minors, built children's libraries or reading rooms according to local conditions, and opened up cultural activity centers especially for children. The government encourages and guides social forces to build children's cultural facilities and centers, to give financial aid to children's cultural activities that are public welfare-oriented. Cultural workers in various places use official national festivals and holidays, traditional festivals and commemoration days to organize cultural activities geared to minors; such activities are held on a public square, community, family, campus and township basis. The government also pays attention to guiding writers and artists to go deep into life, to create literary and artistic works conducive to the healthy growth of minors, and encourages and supports performances for minors.

Culture serves the masses of the people, and it is most important to do a good job in cultural construction in rural China. In 1994, I was transferred from the province to Beijing to serve as Minister of Radio, Film and Television and when I received my letter of appointment, I could not help recalling watching a movie when I was a child. I was born in a remote village which, until I was enrolled into university at the age of 19, I had never left. It was a poverty-stricken area without a cinema; movies were shown in the open air. Adults sat on the ground or on wooden benches, and the children who couldn't see clearly stood on the benches. The first movie I saw was about war. The morning after the screening, a slightly older child came to call me before dawn, saying that so

CULTURE IS LIKE WATER

Entertainment center established by farmers

many guns had been fired the day before, and we should rush off to pick up the shell cases. For me, movies were a very beautiful dream and were the first channel through which I came to know history, outside the village and the world. Watching movies in the open air in those years left me with good memories. In China today, there are many farmers and children in rural areas who still watch in the open. It can be said that they are the most dedicated audiences. And the film industry should never forget them. I still remember that when cultural activities were held in the village, we kids played around under the table. Although conditions at that time were simple and crude and activities were very few, they brought us great delight. Since becoming Minister of Culture, that situation and experience often come to mind. The cultural interests of farmers and migrant workers receive special attention from the Chinese government and cultural circles. At present, we have made the development of rural public cultural services as the focus of our work, and are drawing up relevant plans; on the basis of realizing the goal of establishing cultural clubs and libraries in every county, we have launched the project of building culture centers in towns and townships. Through a combination of central and local funding, we have built, renovated and expanded a large batch of culture centers, and improved the situation of backward cultural facilities in towns and townships. In an effort to eliminate the digital gulf, and real-

Culture is like water

Theatrical performance in a rural area

ize sharing of resources, the Chinese government has launched a project of sharing the nation's cultural resources and information, and have kept expanding the overall amount and scope of cultural resources serving rural areas. We also encourage and support rural traditional cultural activities, tap national and popular traditional cultural resources, organize and develop cultural activities to the liking of the broad masses of farmers. As modernization and urbanization progress, over 100 million farmers have come to the cities for work and protection of their cultural rights and interests has received government attention. The government gives full play to the role of public welfare-related cultural facilities;

guides cultural business units and literary and artistic workers to go into the thick of migrant workers' life, creating and producing programs that reflect their life and are very popular with them; and encourages cultural business units and literary and artistic workers to provide migrant workers with cultural products and services at preferential rates or at no cost at all. Related government departments are also cooperating with common effort to establish effective working mechanisms. At the same time, they promote the cultural construction of the employers of migrant workers; actively support the establishment of performing groups at the units employing migrant workers, develop amateur performance groups of migrant workers, and encourage such workers to create and perform their own entertainment and theatrical programs.

We will intensify cultural exchange with overseas countries, strengthen the heart-to-heart linkage between the people of China and of other countries around the world, and use the best of foreign cultural products and cultural services to enrich the spiritual and cultural life of the Chinese people. The potential of the Chinese cultural market is great, and competition is becoming increasingly fierce. Cultural products that benefit the receivers — particularly the physical and mental health of youngsters — and those that benefit social harmony and world peace are being increasingly welcomed, whilst cultural products that spread pornography and violence are increasingly met with aversion and resistance. Like the cultural ministers of many countries, I think one cannot regard culture merely as a means of earning money, but rather one should use culture to satisfy people's spiritual needs. People's development cannot be achieved by relying solely on material things, and it is my hope that Chinese and foreign businessmen and entrepreneurs engaged in cultural undertakings will listen and respond to public calls for concern for the humanities to meet their cultural needs.

IV.

Culture is like water, which silently seeps into and nurtures all forms of life.

The functions and roles of culture in education, inspiration, molding of character, esthetics and enjoyment are largely manifested in an indirect and profound way, and in subtle, imperceptible change. In this sense, culture is like water, which silently seeps into and nurtures all forms of life.

A harmonious society is the environment for citizens' harmonious life, and the foundation for people's all-round development. Guided by the scientific development outlook, China puts great emphasis on the coordinated development of economy, politics, culture and society, and on the status and role of culture as it fuses into economy and politics in the overall national strength. Cultural construction is an important dimension of carrying out scientific development as well as the cultural underpinning for realizing the scientific development outlook. The Chinese government's support for cultural construction is an embodiment of the cultural-awareness of establishing oneself in the vanguard of the times. In recent years, cultural construction has been incorporated into the development plans and construction goals of central and local governments and the active role of culture permeates every aspect of social life. The cultural development situation is gratifying as never before.

Chinese cultural circles will consciously shoulder their cultural responsibility in the construction of a harmonious society. Adherence to the people-based scientific development outlook in building a harmonious socialist society unfolds bright and happy prospects before the Chinese people and China's cultural construction takes this as its own value orientation. Building a prosperous, democratic and civilized modern socialist state is the social goal of cultural construction; its educational goal is to promote people's all-round development and to train socialist citizens with high ideals, moral integrity, a good education and a strong sense of discipline. These two goals serve as mutual prerequisites and complements, and are unified in the practice of building socialism with Chinese characteristics. Modern China's cultural construction should center closely round these goals, and should be implemented widely and deeply.

The essence of culture is man's outward development, a reflection of people's existence, thinking, capabilities and aspirations, and a product of mankind's creative thinking. The object upon which culture acts is humanity itself, determining men's qualities and abilities, the style and state of their existence. It is precisely for this reason that China's cultural construction always sets its sights on satisfying people's growing spiritual and cultural needs, and on improving the ideological and moral qualities and the scientific and cultural competence of the whole nation. Under the condition of a market economy, it is important to prevent an over-simplified and pragmatic approach to culture and arts.

The basic strategy of China's cultural construction is founded on having a correct grasp of the demand of our times and on the basic national condition. In the first 20 years of the new millennium, a series of major changes will occur in various dimensions of China's social and economic life, but three basic aspects of modern Chinese society will not change: First, China is a developing country, and even when the goal of building a well-off society in an all-round way is achieved China will still be in the primary stage of socialism; second, the western region and some less developed areas will experience tremendous changes through implementation of the strategy for western development and the building of a new socialist countryside, but China's regional differences and backwardness in some regions will

■ Water-Releasing Festival held during the Pure Brightness Festival at the Dujiang Weir in Guanxian County, Sichuan Province

Nadam Fair of the Mongolian people

persist for a long time to come; third, comprehensive construction of a well-off society requires the coordinated development of economy, politics and culture, but making economic construction the central task will remain a crucial issue to which we must cling fast. On this basis, we call for the focus of cultural work to be on construction and valuing accreted experience. Cultural construction is a gradual process of development amidst accreted experience and of innovation amidst development. We have put forward five major tasks, namely: strengthening construction in cultural ideology theory; construction in the ranks of talents, construction in the legal system and institutions, construction in infrastructure and construction in cultural work. The first four tasks are a kind of guarantee system, and fall within the remit of government; cultural work construction belongs to the construction of culture *per se*. It needs the creative labor of cultural and artistic workers. The government encourages the independent creative spirit and protects the display of this kind of creativity according to law.

The basic elements of culture can be divided into four aspects — knowledge, sentiment, social ethics and belief. These four aspects infiltrate one another, forming an open, relatively independent and continuously developing system. Observing these four aspects in terms of the cultural structure system, we find that Chinese culture in the new period, alongside the development of Chinese society, is experiencing profound changes and is breeding another period of development and renewal.

— The information technology revolution has brought huge changes in the field of cognition, and injected strong vitality and vigor into economic development and social progress. At the same time, it has broken the internal equilibrium of the traditional cultural structure system, thereby creating the necessity and possibility for cultural development and renewal. Knowledge comprising a range of cognitive content from information to science is the outermost and most superficial level, and the level of rapid and frequent changes.

With the arrival of the information age, there has been explosive growth in information and knowledge, enormously widening people's cognitive realm and exerting positive influence on the liberation of social productivity; at the same time, it has strongly infiltrated people's emotional world and social ethics. Information technology has not only created a strong transmission system, but has hastened the birth of brand-new cultural forms. New science and technology have brought novelty and stimulation, as well as confusion and puzzlement. Information is the foundation for and the primary link in people's understanding of the world. But information does not equal knowledge, knowledge does not equal wisdom, and wisdom does not equal ability. A swarm of disorderly information can become knowledge only through effective reception, identification and integration, thereby really entering the realm of culture. Knowledge can be handed along, but wisdom and ability cannot. Wisdom and ability can be acquired only through people's practice and summary, their experience and comprehension. In brief, modern developments and advances in science and technology have not only set out requirements for the development and innovation of culture, but have also provided the possibility for such development and innovation in terms of content, form and means. People are justified in expressing their worries about the various negative phenomena that have come with the information age, but we should not and cannot reject modern developments and advances in science and technology. Worrying alone will not help. Promoting what is beneficial

Guzang Festival of the Miao people

and avoiding what is harmful is the only correct choice.

— Economic development and social progress have inspired people's spirit, and reinforced confidence in creating a new life, whilst fierce competition, complex interest relationships and the endless emergence of new situations and new problems have also caused a certain restlessness and uneasiness in people's emotional worlds. Construction of a harmonious society calls for concern for humanities. The sentiment in the cultural system is people's perceived value judgment on and reflection of natural and social life; its symbolic form is literature and art. Sentiment exerts a profound influence on social ethics and belief. In a period of restructuring and great social change, culture, as the banner of na-

Water-sprinkling Festival of the Dai people in Yunnan Province

Culture is like water

tional spirit, plays an important guiding role in society. The functions of literature and art in soothing and stimulating people's minds are especially prominent. The reform, opening-up and modernization drive has brought about tremendous change in the lives of the Chinese people in their advance from a basic comfortable life to all-round prosperity. The development history of some countries has shown that the stage in which per-capita gross national product (GNP) rises from US$1,000 to US$3,000 may be the period of accelerating economic development, and at the same time a period of striking social contradictions. Society advances toward an ideal state precisely through the process of continuously solving problems arising from development. Chinese society is in this kind of development period right now. Only when literary and artistic workers go deeply into life, into reality and into people's inner worlds, can they be the conscience of society, and create works that touch people, thereby creating a cultural context conducive to the building of a harmonious society.

— Spiritual civilization has been given attention, ideological and moral education has been further strengthened, but the losing of cultural roots and fault lines in the social ethics and morality stratum remain serious phenomena. The construction of a moral standard system in tune with a socialist market economy, coordinated with socialist legal norms and perpetuating the traditional virtues of the Chinese people is an onerous task and long process. Social ethics is the code of conduct of a group of people; its essence is to restrain and regulate relations between people and between people and society. Such restraint and regulation are realized mainly through laws and morality. Law is an external rule and involves compulsion; while morality is discipline from the self, relying mainly on self-awareness. The French political thinker Montesquieu said that law is the most fundamental morality, while morality is the highest law. In traditional Chinese culture, social ethics is most developed. Ancient ethics classified complex social relationships into five categories, namely, king - minister, father - son, husband - wife, elder - younger brothers and friends, and extended this to others by parity of reasoning. The ancient philosopher Xunzi expanded the ethical concept to the relationship between man and nature, saying that etiquette has three foundations: Heaven and earth as the foundation of life; ancestry as the foundation of class; kingship as the foundation of rule. The principles of ancient ethics were guaranteed by very complete ceremonial and standards; at the same time, through the vehicle of culture and in forms welcomed by the public, these principles spread through and permeated society, passing down from generation to generation. There is a familiar saying "The tree wants to remain quiet, but the wind won't stop." In fact, this saying was originally used to express ethical feelings. Once Confucius heard his follower Gao Yu weeping and wailing, and when he asked why, Gao answered through his tears, "The tree wants to

National Cultural Information and Resources Sharing Project is a government project to bridge the digital divide.

remain quiet, but the wind won't stop; the son wants to support his parents in their old age, but they are already gone." This sentence that blends emotion and reason still touches people's hearts when they read it more than two thousand years later. In the aspect of social ethics and morality, various reasons past and current have led to the emergence of the phenomena of losing cultural roots and fault lines in culture. The Chinese government pays great attention to the continuation of excellent traditions in the advance of modernization and to the reconstruction of morality under market conditions. At present, education on the socialist "honor and shame concept" is being carried out in breadth and depth.

This work needs to be pressed forward in a persistent way.

— Belief is man's spiritual pillar. The carriers of belief are religion and philosophy. China's Constitution protects citizens' freedom to believe or not believe in religion. For the majority of the Chinese, beliefs are mostly embodied in a kind of cultural value system. The mutual consideration given between belief and reality and the rebuilding of the value system of the whole nation are problems needing intensive studies and solutions in theory and practice. Who am I? Where do I come from? Where am I going? What is the ultimate significance of life? These problems have lingered in people's hearts and minds since the dawn of human society.

The theater stage in Huguang Guild Hall in Beijing

With the inner support of a value system and the far-off light of a guiding ideal, real life starts to have meaning. People need inspiration in real life, at the same time, they are punctiliously pursuing ultimate solicitude. That is the mission of culture. How to closely integrate ideals with realities and persevere in properly carrying out construction of a value system centered on scientific belief is cultural construction's most important task. The enhancement of our people's qualities and the establishment of scientific belief are a gradual cultural process, one that calls for long-term effort.

The world is becoming ever more inter-connected, and just as our planet shares coolness and warmth, so the rise or fall and the withering or flourishing of cultures cannot be cut off from mutual influence. We should proceed from China's reality and, with our own courage, wisdom and ability, jointly face up to all opportunities and difficulties in the development of world culture. In our opinion, when we shoulder cultural responsibility for our own country, we are also actually undertaking responsibility on behalf of human society.

V.

Mother culture is our root, and the foundation for creating new culture.

Culture is Like Water

> We should cherish a kind of reverence before the heritage created by our ancestors. This is our mother culture, our root, and the foundation for creating new culture. The more rapid the period of social development the more important it is that people should not lose their memories, the more important it is that they should not forget the road home.

The Mogao Grottoes in Dunhuang, Gansu Province, already on the World Cultural Heritage list and world-famous as a pearl of Oriental art, is an "art gallery in the desert." Several generations of cultural relics protection workers have carried out protection and research work here in extremely tough living and working conditions; day in day out, year in year out, they have held fast to the grottoes, their achievements have gone down in history, their spirit moving one to tears or to singing their praises. They are representatives of the vast number of cultural relics workers of modern China and are the epitome of many generations of Chinese people defending their spiritual homeland. When I paid an inspection visit there, I wrote down the above lines in response to a request by the head of the State Cultural Relics Bureau. My friend, a composer, kindly put the lines to music. In 2005, the meeting of the World Cultural Heritage Specialist Committee was held in Xi'an, Shaanxi Province, and a group of Chinese children sang this song. Although the poem was ordinary, it evoked sighs from Chinese and foreign cultural relics experts attending the meeting. Perhaps, the children's

The National Museum of China

young voices stirred up associations and sighs, causing them to taste once more the mix of emotions involved in the protection of cultural heritage — sweetness, bitterness, desolation, sadness and joy.

How to properly handle relations between the preservation of cultural heritage and the construction of a new life, leaving behind memories that should not be forgotten in mankind's journey to the future is a world problem in need of urgent solution. In the long process of history, many world heritage sites have been subjected to constant erosion over years, while war, theft and illegal trafficking in cultural relics have also brought many valuable heritages to the verge of extinction. At the same time, in the process of building a new life, man has wrought shocking destruction on his heritage due to inadequate understanding and erroneous work. The 5,000-year civilized history of the Chinese people has left an extremely rich legacy of cultural heritage. There is

Culture is like water

The Mogao Grottoes in Dunhuang, the greatest repository of Buddhist art

Culture is like water

"tangible" cultural heritage in material form - such as cultural relics, ancient books and records. There is also "intangible" cultural heritage in non-material form that is passed down predominantly by oral teaching and which is rich in content and diverse in form; this includes oral traditions, performing arts, social practices, rituals and festive events and traditional craftsmanship. The "tangible" and 'intangible" material and non-material parts of cultural heritage jointly constitute the integral whole of a people's cultural heritage and none of them can be dispensed with. Strengthening Chinese cultural heritage protection is a necessity for the development of the country and people, a necessity for safeguarding world cultural diversity, and an essential requirement for civilized dialogue among the international community and for the sustainable development of human society.

Cultural heritage represents the blood vessels by which a people's culture is transmitted; it cannot be cut off; cultural heritage is also the foundation for carrying forward the spirit of a people and creating new culture; it must not be weakened. Cultural heritage represents the only conduit between ourselves and our distant ancestors, and rare material evidence left by the splendid history of humankind. National and folk cultures are our roots and the wellspring of cultural development. Along with the development of society, tracing back one's roots is a universal desire among mankind. To treasure cultural heritage is not just to reflect upon the distant past; it is a necessity in order to create new culture.

As modernization develops, the quickening pace of social progress implies a similar acceleration in the new replacing the old. Generally speaking, history is moving forward and human society is also making constant progress. But a concrete analysis of literature and art reveals that we cannot say in a simplified way that one generation excels another generation; the high peaks created by our forebears naturally had their own epochal conditions and historical imperatives, and more often than not, we cannot surpass them. We can only create our own high peaks on the basis of those our forebears created. The development of literature and art is not a stepped progress of continual surpassing; rather it represents a forest of high peaks, each with their own merits. Even though there is inheritance and development in the growth of science and technology, there have been losses too. For this reason, some ancient technological achievements are beyond the reach of modern man. Therefore, we should cherish reverence for the things created by our ancestors, including exquisite ethnic and folk cultures. These are our mother culture and our roots. The more rapid the period of social development the more important it is that people should not lose their memories, the more important it is that they should not forget the road home. It is very important to protect existing historical heritage and the memories of our ancestors. Only when we are clear about where we come from can we advance toward the future with firmer steps and stronger self-confidence.

Culture is like water

Terracotta warriors and horses excavated in Xi'an, dubbed "the Eighth Wonder of the World"

Culture is like water

In recent years, China has striven to expand the scope of protection work and has thus achieved important progress in the protection of cultural relics. In putting into practice the principle of "protection as the leading factor, letting rescue come first, reasonable utilization and strengthening management," we have strengthened legislation on the protection of cultural relics, promulgated the Law on the Protection of Cultural Relics, revised the Regulations on Implementation of the Law on the Protection of Cultural Relics, and actively promoted local legislative work on cultural relics. In 2005, the State Council transmitted to subordinate departments the document the Notice on Strengthening Protection of Cultural Heritage. In 2006, it designated the second Saturday in June every year as China's Cultural Heritage Day; the theme of the first Cultural Heritage Day was to "Protect cultural heritage, and guard the spiritual homeland." Currently there are 2,352 key cultural relics protection units across China. Cultural relics administrative law-enforcement institutions at all levels have been gradually set up and telling blows have been dealt to illegal and criminal activities such as excavation for theft and smuggling of cultural relics. Various items of basic verification work have been reinforced, trial work in establishing archive in cultural relics units under national protection and construction of a database system are progressing smoothly; and the security of cultural relics in museum collections has been strengthened. Protection of large sites is in full swing, and one important site after another has been listed as world cultural heritage. On the one hand, we have chosen the most quintessential relics to be displayed at exhibitions abroad; on the other, we have extensively invited representative cultural heritage sites of the world to hold exhibitions in China. These international exchanges have become most effective windows for enhancing friendship and understanding between China and foreign countries.

Putting the protection of non-material heritage as an important element of national and folk culture high on the agenda represents breakthrough progress in cultural heritage protection. The Chinese government has promulgated the Opinion on Strengthening the Protection Work Related to Chinese Non-Material Cultural Heritage, clearly defining the guiding principle, goals, work approaches and various guarantee measures for the protection of non-material cultural heritage, and pushed forward application for and establishment of the listing of the first batch of representative works of national non-material cultural heritage. So far, China's Kunqu opera, *guqin* (a seven stringed plucked instrument) art, Uygur Muqam art of Xinjiang and Inner Mongolian "long tune" folk song have been selected and listed among UNESCO's "Masterpieces of the Oral and Intangible Heritage of Humanity." The government and related institutions and organizations have done much highly fruitful work in the investigation, collation, research and protection of non-material cultural heritage.

The implementation of the "Chinese national and folk cultural protection project" receives high attention from central government down to local government level. China has formally acceded to the "Convention on the Means of Prohibiting and Preventing the Illicit Import, Export and Transfer of Ownership of Cultural Property" and the "Convention for the Safeguarding of the Intangible Cultural Heritage" and other international conventions relating to the protection of cultural heritage, thus laying the foundation for promoting international cooperation in protection work related to non-material cultural heritage. In 2006, the State Council published 518 items on the list of the first batch of national non-material heritage, thus creating a precedent for the protection of non-material heritage by listing; traditional festivals have also been incorporated into the list of state-level protection. The Law on the Protection of Non-Material Heritage has also been included in the 2007 legislation plan of the National People's Congress.

Museums are a very important indicator for judging a country's cultural development. When I visited the United States, my hosts once put me up in the Metropolitan Museum and once in the Museum of Radio, Television and Film. What is a museum? A museum is a place to "treasure up history and signal the future," a museum is a citizen's lifelong school. China presently has 2,300 museums of various types. We encourage popular and social forces to run museums and have thus greatly promoted the development of the museum undertaking. Every year a total of nearly 10,000 exhibitions has been held, which receive about 150 million

A Dunhuang mural Tang Dynasty Orchestra

CULTURE IS LIKE WATER

visitors from China and from abroad by turnstile count; some museums have made rapid improvements in their infrastructure, research and display, management, operation and social services, catching up with or approaching the advanced international level. We will try to bring museums closer to the public through various measures, so that visiting museums after work becomes a national habit across China.

■ Simuwu four-legged vessel, famous bronze ware of the Shang Dynasty

■ Famille rose porcelain vase with reticulated exterior and revolving interior, Qing Dynasty

■ Jade dragon excavated at the Neolithic Hongshan Culture Site, regarded as China's earliest

■ Chinese Tourism symbol — Galloping Horse Treading on a Flying Swallow, bronze ware, Eastern Han Dynasty

Intensifying the protection of cultural heritage is closely related to the scientific development road that China is following. At present, in the context where the world puts too much stress on economic development, for various social and economic reasons, culture as the intangible heritage

Culture is like water

of mankind is ebbing away. Cultural desertification will cause the economic oasis to lose its spiritual support. Over their long history, the Chinese people of various ethnic groups have together created precious cultural heritage, rare in the world for its multiplicity of types, diversity of forms and wealth of content. Therefore, protecting China's cultural heritage is a responsibility placed upon our shoulders by history. In this we have a strong sense of mission and awareness of responsibility; we take up this historical responsibility, retain the special character of our national memory and properly protect our spiritual homeland. When people go all out after economic development to get rid of poverty, they are often apt to neglect protection of the environment, to ignore verdant hills and streams and clear river water; they are often apt to neglect cultural construction, to ignore our ancestors' cultural remains and people's spiritual homeland. Once having achieved a rich material life, looking around and recalling the past, they often discover it is hard to avoid many regrets and it is too late to repent; such deep lessons can often be seen in human history.

Time waits for no man in the protection of cultural heritage; we are working against the clock. Cultural heritage, being rich in content and diverse in form, requires different ideas and ways of protection. China did a great deal of work and scored initial results in the rescue and protection of cul-

China's non-material cultural heritage — *guqin*, seven-stringed plucked instrument

Culture is like water

tural heritage during the 20th century. But we should look at things soberly and recognize that a grim situation still exists in China's work of cultural heritage protection. How to properly handle the relationship between the modernization drive and the protection of cultural heritage is a big and difficult issue. In the process of industrialization and urbanization, we should not sacrifice the precious assets left to us by our ancestors, nor should we engage in destructive "cultural relics exploitation" along the lines of "burning a famous harp for fuel and cooking a crane for meat." In regard to the protection of non-material cultural heritage, the current outstanding problems are: one, the rapid change in the ecological environment upon which China's non-material cultural heritage relies for its survival and the serious situation of loss of resources, the lack of worthy successors — some traditional techniques are faced with extinction; two, statute construction is still to be accelerated, and non-material cultural heritage has not been protected according to law; three, cultural heritage protection awareness still needs to be improved; four, protection mechanisms urgently need improvement, etc.

"Stones from other hills may polish the jade" and in the protection of China's cultural heritage, we actively participate in international cooperation and exchange, learning from and drawing on the advanced protection experience of other countries; at the same time, we are willing to let other coun-

Tangka, age-old Tibetan Buddhist art

Culture is like water

CULTURE IS LIKE WATER

tries share our experience. We are exploring a way with Chinese characteristics for the protection of cultural heritage, and that might provide useful references for the protection of world cultural heritage. In 2005, China held an international forum with "traditional culture and modernization" as the theme, devoted to the study and discussion of the interaction of traditional culture and modernization, and strengthening exchange of useful experience, and cooperation carried out by various countries in the rescue, protection and development of traditional culture. At that meeting, I stated:

▎ China's non-material cultural heritage — Uygur Muqam art of Xinjiang

China's non-material cultural heritage — Kunqu opera

— In the surging tide of modernization, paying attention to the rescue and protection of traditional culture, in particular important cultural heritage and excellent national and folk cultural art, has become a very urgent and important task. The accelerating process of modernization has caused different degrees of damage and increasingly rapid loss of traditional cultures of various countries worldwide. Such loss would affect the balance of the cultural ecology as would the extinction of many species affect the natural ecological environment; furthermore, it would fetter man's creativity, restrict the sustainable development of the economy and all-round progress of society. The protection and development of traditional culture traces back to the roots of various national cultures and provides rich resources for present and future cultural development. Therefore, it has

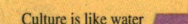

Culture is like water

become the common view of many countries, that in the process of modernization one should protect native culture, encourage cultural diversity, enhance a sense of identification with national culture and a sense of ownership so as to promote virtuous interaction in promoting the protection of cultural resources and the cultural eco-environment; and that one should prevent blind and destructive development prompted by anxiety for quick success and instant benefits. The Chinese government pays great attention to the protection of traditional culture, and is willing to exchange with various countries experiences and lessons in this respect, to explore methods for international cooperation and to propel continuous advancement in the protection of traditional culture.

— The protection of traditional culture includes both traditional culture in material form and traditional culture in a non-material form. At present, domestic legislation on the protection of material cultural heritages and mechanisms for international collaboration have become fairly complete, but as regards to the protection of non-material cultural heritage, there are still very few countries that have special domestic legislation, and international cooperation is very insufficient. It is hoped that while attention is paid to the protection of material cultural heritage, more concern will be shown to the expansion and strengthening of international exchange and cooperation in the protection of non-material cultural heritage.

— The rescue and protection of traditional culture in the process of modernization not only involves a conceptual problem; more importantly, it is a question of method. We should jointly explore concrete solutions to the problem of conflicts that arise between the modernization process and traditional culture; in particular, we should do creative work in regard to the main measures for the protection of traditional culture, the pattern and practice of legislation relating to non-material cultural heritage, mechanisms for international cooperation and exchange and other concrete operational aspects.

— The government should play a key role in the protection of traditional culture; it is necessary to study how government should realize cultural inheritance and innovation through policy readjustment. Governments of various countries should take a responsible attitude toward history in dealing with the protection of traditional culture, so as to make it a reliable sample version of history, by which people understand the past. Governments of various countries should also have traditional culture adapt itself to modern society and have the residual fine spiritual cultural heritage in traditional culture serve modern life. Inheriting traditional culture in the process of development, encouraging innovation amid inheritance, so that it meets the needs of modern society and of modern people's spiritual life ...these likewise are urgent tasks facing governments of various countries in carrying out cultural construction at the present time.

Culture is like water

The Jiayu Pass in Gansu Province, situated on the Silk Road

Culture is like water

The abundant cultural resources of the Chinese people are an important component of world cultural heritage. Protecting and developing traditional culture in the process of modernization not only concerns harmony and equality among different civilizations and different cultures, but also has to do with the common fate and future of humankind. We are willing to undertake this mission incumbent upon us, members of this generation, together with the people of various countries around the world. Early in 2006, I met with Rocco Buttiglione, Italy's minister of cultural heritage activity and the vice-foreign minister Alfredo Mantica in Beijing. I said at that meeting that over the past few years we had all along been striving to apply for inclusion of the "Silk Road" on the world heritage list, because there are many historical sites along the Chinese section, including the ancient cities of Jiaohe and Loulan. But, I thought, a road invariably has a starting point and an ending. The starting point of the "Silk Road" was Xi'an in China and though it went through many places after reaching Europe, its central terminal was still Rome, from where it radiated to other places in Europe. So I proposed that China and Italy jointly apply for inclusion of the "Silk Road" on the world heritage list, because one end of the "Silk Road" — the central starting point — was in Xi'an, and the other end — the central terminal point — was in Rome. Through this project, it would be possible to closely link China and Italy together, just as the "Silk Road" had done. My proposal was warmly received by my Italian friends.

VI.

Chinese cultural tradition contains a kind of ideological vigor and spirit of innovation that ceaselessly reproduces and renews itself.

"It is a long, very long road, I will go up and down along it in search of the things I want." These lines by the famous poet Qu Yuan written more than 2,000 years ago, have resounded throughout the long history of the Chinese people. Chinese cultural tradition contains a kind of ideological vigor and spirit of innovation that ceaselessly reproduces and renews itself.

Culture is a living form unique to mankind, and since innovation is the essential characteristic of culture, culture is also an important way for mankind to realize his own value. Today's China, with freedom of ideas and a broad and open mind, is in an age when cultural innovation is in full swing; the broad cultural expression and surging cultural innovation will be a spiritual cornerstone of the future well-off society at a higher level; they will also be the deep motive force driving forward the great rejuvenation of the Chinese people, and the wellspring maintaining the exuberant vitality of our ancient motherland.

There are complex reasons for the formation of cultural tradition of a country or a society. Once the tradition is formed and is quite stable in character and capable of being passed down, it becomes a strong force for cohesion. At the same time, any kind of culture should be an open system; only by continuous adjustment and renewal along with epochal development and social change can it always retain vitality and vigor that grow with the passing years.

Proceeding from the goal of building a people-based harmonious society, the Chinese government is implementing the principle of respecting knowledge, talent, labor and creation throughout society in a more conscientious and more conspicuous way, carrying out the national strategy of independent innovation, and paying great attention to cultural innovation. It states the whole innovation system should be determined together by cultural innovation and theoretical innovation, system innovation and science and technology innovation. Cultural innovation concerns not just the development of culture itself; it has even more bearing on the socialist modernization drive as a whole and on the future of our people. Accordingly, the Chinese government has consistently continued its unremitting efforts against criminal piracy and smuggling, for the protection of intellectual property rights and the protection of national cultural creativity.

In cultural construction, stress should be laid on stability and accreted experience, developing in stability and innovating in the context of accreted experience. The cream of Chinese cultural tradition includes ancient cultural traditions more than 2,000 years old, includes the patriotic, democratic, and scientific tradition formed in the New Culture Movement that started in 1916 and the revolutionary and socialist cultural traditions formed under the leadership of the Communist Party of China (CPC). That is a valuable spiritual asset. At the same time, one should be aware that wheat and chaff always coexist in a tradition, and that even an excellent tradition needs to undergo constant transformation and renewal, acquiring new connotations and vigor so as to keep abreast of the times.

Endless innovation is the distinctive characteristic of the vitality of Chinese culture. In world history, one splendid ancient culture after another has been cut off or fallen into oblivion. How is it that Chinese culture can keep going on and has become even newer with the passing of time? Of course, there are many reasons, but the innovation tradition of the Chinese people has an important bearing on this phenomenon. China has always been a country of many ethnic groups who have depended on one another and coexisted since antiquity. The various ethnic group cultures maintain their own distinct character; they absorb and integrate with one another, finally forming one heterogeneous body of Chinese culture — a very strong cohesive, fusing and vital force. China has since ancient times had the tradition of "letting a hundred schools of thought contend," and the various schools and disciplines compare, learn from, contend with and mingle with one another, such activity helping invigorate thinking and stimulate innovation. In essence, Chinese culture is an open system. Our ancestors advocated tolerance by saying "being like the sea which takes in a hundred streams." They were good at learning widely from the strong points of others, and had the courage to undertake self-examination; from exchanges with and by learning from

The Night Banquet in Han Xizai's Mansion, a Five Dynasties (907-960) period painting

different countries, they constantly enriched and developed themselves. Even though in modern times they experienced a period when the country was closed off from the outside world, they never stopped facing the world nor their exploration and struggle for self-improvement and new progress. Chinese cultural tradition contains a kind of ideological vigor and spirit of innovation that ceaselessly reproduces and renews itself. This ideological vigor and innovative spirit are in the bloodstream of the entire people and this is why they have tenacious vitality despite having been oppressed and suffocated in the shackles of feudal rule. Precisely because of his, the Chinese people can continuously realize its own transformation and renewal along with epochal changes. With the beginning of the new millennium, China has entered the new historical period of building a well-off society in an all-round way. Modern Chinese culture is a reflection of the life of the modern Chinese society and exerts positive influence on social development and progress. The economic base and social life upon which Chinese culture relies for its growth and development have and still are experiencing profound change. Therefore, cultural construction and innovation are no longer succession and continuation in the ordinary sense, rather, they are the transformation and reshaping of traditional culture in a modernization direction; they are continuous creation and renewal proceeding from its original connotation to expanded notion.

In the last analysis, the flourishing of culture and art

depends upon the enthusiasm and creativity of writers, artists and cultural workers. Innovation implies reflecting on traditional concepts and exploration of unknown spheres; it calls for strong imagination and creativity, for innovative thinking and unique ways of expression. Innovation will also be accompanied by discussion and contention between different schools of thought and different academic viewpoints. The process of innovation is a process of experimentation, one in which shortcomings or mistakes are inevitable. All the fruits of innovation have to be tested by practice and history.

An artistic masterpiece represents the spiritual heights and the cultural profundity that a people or an epoch can reach, can bring about a substantive rise in the level of citizens' cultural life and act as an impetus for the overall development of cultural construction. Therefore, it is also the major target which cultural innovation assiduously seeks. Great works that will be handed down from age to age is the aspiration of all writers and artists with lofty ideals; even more, it demonstrates man's endless pursuit of beauty. One's lifespan is limited, "as fragile as grass and trees," but the classics are immortal, with "a fame surpassing the hardness of metal and stone." Artists of today's China, like the ancients, have the determination to "trace perseveringly after the remote past," hoping that their finite lives will merge into the infinity of history, hoping to achieve transcendence over individual life. This historical sentiment of artists is a motive

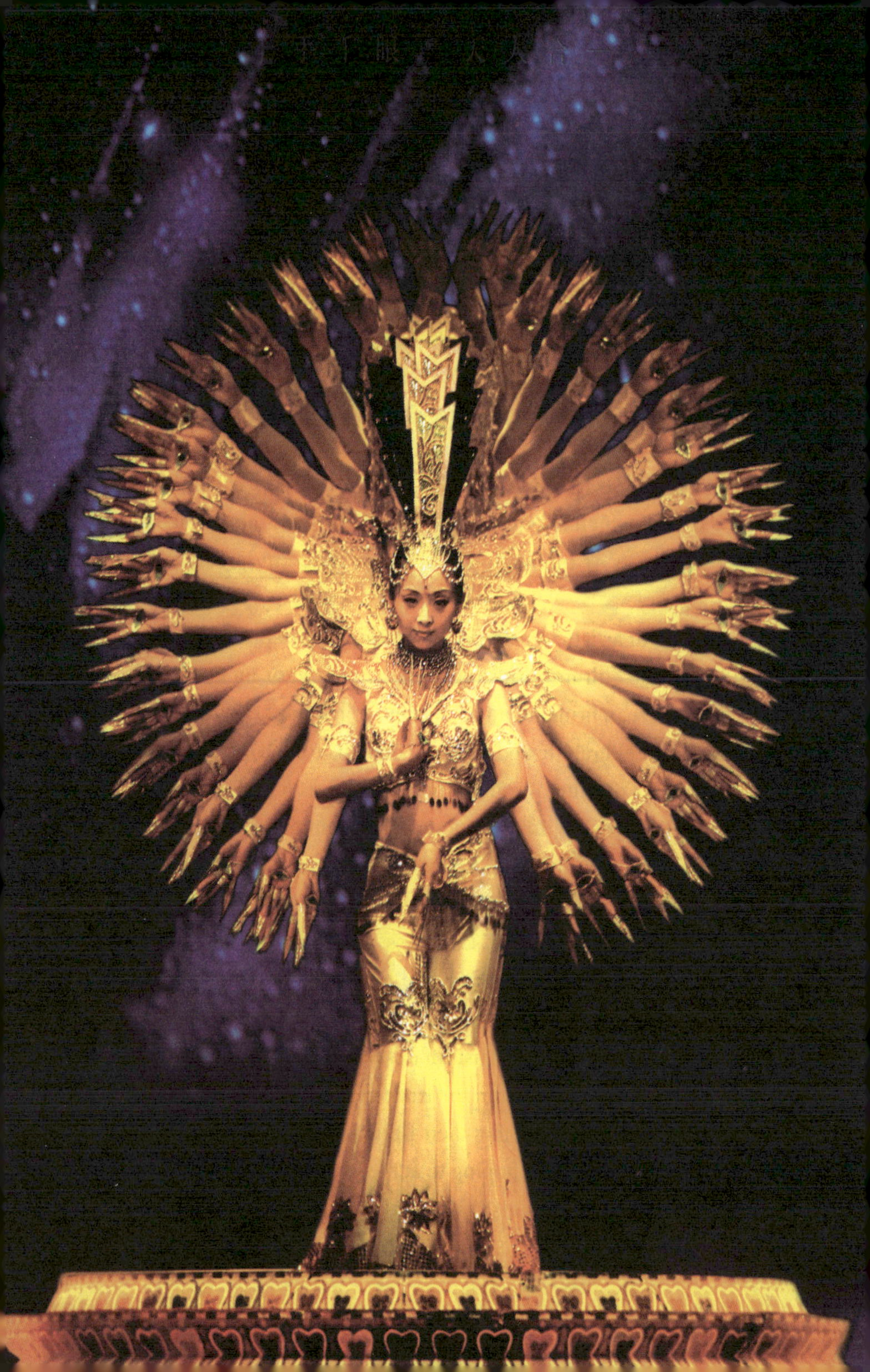

power propelling the advance of culture and art. China's several millennia-long history has left us many excellent cultural products, and even in this age of fast-food culture, many excellent cultural works have come to the fore. In the new context of initiating the scientific development outlook, the driving force of the pursuit of outstanding works of art is not only a fresh manifestation of artists' responsibility to the age, to the people, and to the future, but is also rich in connotations for the sustainable development of culture. Master works are the strongest link in the chain of culture and arts development, they are the cream of cultural creation and have the richest cultural accretion. All efforts made for the creation of excellent works in an era will become an important foundation for cultural development.

In 1998, shortly after I came to work with the Ministry of Culture, that year's National Art Creation Conference was held in Dali City, Yunnan Province. The movie *Five Golden Flowers* was produced at this popular beauty spot several decades ago, and is so familiar to ordinary people that even today they still can relate its story in detail. In March in Dali, butterflies were flying by the spring, and in the hearts of those at the conference the idea swelled up of creating more works that would pass down the ages. I stated at the conference that our artistic creation must keep its sights on the dis-

Thousand-Handed Guanyin, performed by the China Disabled People's Performance Art Troupe

tant future, so that our works can enjoy both short-term fame but can also be handed down to future generations. In recent years, China has initiated and implemented the National Excellent Theatrical Artistic Product Project, clearly stipulating as a judgment criterion that a work should enjoy common appreciation irrespective of different locality and times.

 Since the launch of reform and opening-up, many gratifying and inspiring changes have taken place in the situation of China's literary and artistic creation and there are more and more people who are passionate about writing and art. The Internet has provided an infinity of space for art lovers in various trades and professions to display their talent. In terms of quantity, artistic creation has seen geometric growth. People clearly feel that these days, the creation of various kinds of arts has become increasingly lively and a great number of excellent works have emerged, thus enriching people's spiritual life. But some of this flourishing appears too much and too jumbled and some development a little rash. The present state of literature and art is still not satisfactory when compared with the mass of people's growing spiritual needs. The cultural phenomenon is, of course, a complex one, but the lack of understanding of real life, estrangement from the feelings of ordinary people and the lack of human concern for spiritual life must be regarded as the main reasons why currently some works lack artistic appeal. Therefore, we stress the need to persist in getting close to reality, to life and to the masses, to always regard serving the public and the grass-roots level as the starting point and end result of cultural work, and to guide cultural workers in maintaining flesh-and-blood ties with the masses of the people. In creative work, we encourage cultural workers to plunge themselves into the life of the people, to reflect the essence of modern life, to give expression to the pleasures, angers, sorrows and joys of the public, and to create new famous brands in modern Chinese culture. We encourage writers and artists to "let one hundred flowers blossom," to determine on innovation, to guard against and prevent a superficial attitude to life and the withering of artistic imagination.

Brand name strategy is the essence of excellent product strategy. Vigorously creating brand names of excellent national culture is a kind of conscious idea and method that we have gradually become clear about and intensified in recent years. In future cultural construction, it is an especially urgent task for us to enhance our independent innovation ability, and it is very important to create brand names of excellent national culture that possess national characteristics and Chinese style and reflect contemporary spirit. We encourage free development of different forms and styles of artistic creation, and free discussion of different viewpoints and schools of thought in artistic theory; encourage a favorable atmosphere of respect for artistic creation across all society, respect for artistic creation rights, and respect for the fruits of artistic creation. We also regulate relations between government, art production institutions and artistic workers;

we establish artistic innovation mechanisms for active participation in creation by different parties, mechanisms that give powerful guidance and effective stimulation, and are lively and orderly. We will begin with intensifying innovation awareness, perfecting the innovation system and training innovative personnel. We will produce excellent works possessing strong artistic appeal that can be handed down from age to age; form cultural research fruits that have scientific thinking, real knowledge and deep insight; train artistic personnel who have wide reputations and market appeal; create cultural institutions enjoying high reputations at home and abroad and capable of representing the cultural and artistic level of modern China; and hold cultural and artistic activities with first rate operations and extensive influence at home and abroad.

Excellent artistic products and cultural brand names of other countries around the world are also treasured by the Chinese people, who take great interest in cultural innovation work by different countries. The "Year of Russia" and "Year of China" are held by Russia and China respectively in the other's country, and culture is heavily represented in these activities. Before the "Year of Russia" was held, the then Russian Minister of Culture and now head of the Administration of Culture and Film, solicited my ideas about it. My suggestion contained four points, namely, "reproduce classics, display modernity, stress communication and deepen friendship." Russian literary and artistic classics are famous throughout the world, When the Chinese first came in touch with Russian literary and artistic classics, it was the golden age of friendly cooperation between the two countries, so "reproducing the classics" would not only be an artistic pleasure, but would also arouse happy memories of friendly exchange. In relation to this state of mind, the Chinese people are keenly interested in Russia's modern artistic development and cultural creation, therefore, the content should include "displaying modernity." With understanding of a people's cultural history and cultural creation, we could attain the goal of "stressing communication" and "deepening friendship," and lay sound cultural, popular and psychological foundations for strategic partnership between the two countries.

Chinese artists and cultural entrepreneurs pay great attention to foreign experience in artistic creation and market operations, and actively pursue learning from each other and cooperation. For instance, China is a major country for acrobatics and frequently wins gold medals in world contests. The Sun Circus Troupe of Canada is a typical example of a highly successful commercial operation. Chinese artists have taken active part in Sun Circus Troupe events; likewise, Canadians participated in designing of "Time and Space Travel," a program jointly produced by the China Foreign Cultural Group Company and Shanghai artists. We expect that writers and artists and cultural entrepreneurs of different countries will produce more excellent works, create more artistic brand names, jointly enriching the world's cultural treasure house.

Protecting intellectual property rights is the prerequisite for respecting knowledge, respecting talent, respecting labor and respecting creation, and is an important guarantee for carrying out cultural innovation. In recent years, the efforts made and results achieved by the Chinese government in this respect have been clear to all. It was not under pressure that China adopted resolute measures to crack down on piracy and to safeguard intellectual property rights; rather it did so out of conscious de-

■ Beijing opera *The Prosperity of High Tang*

Culture is like water

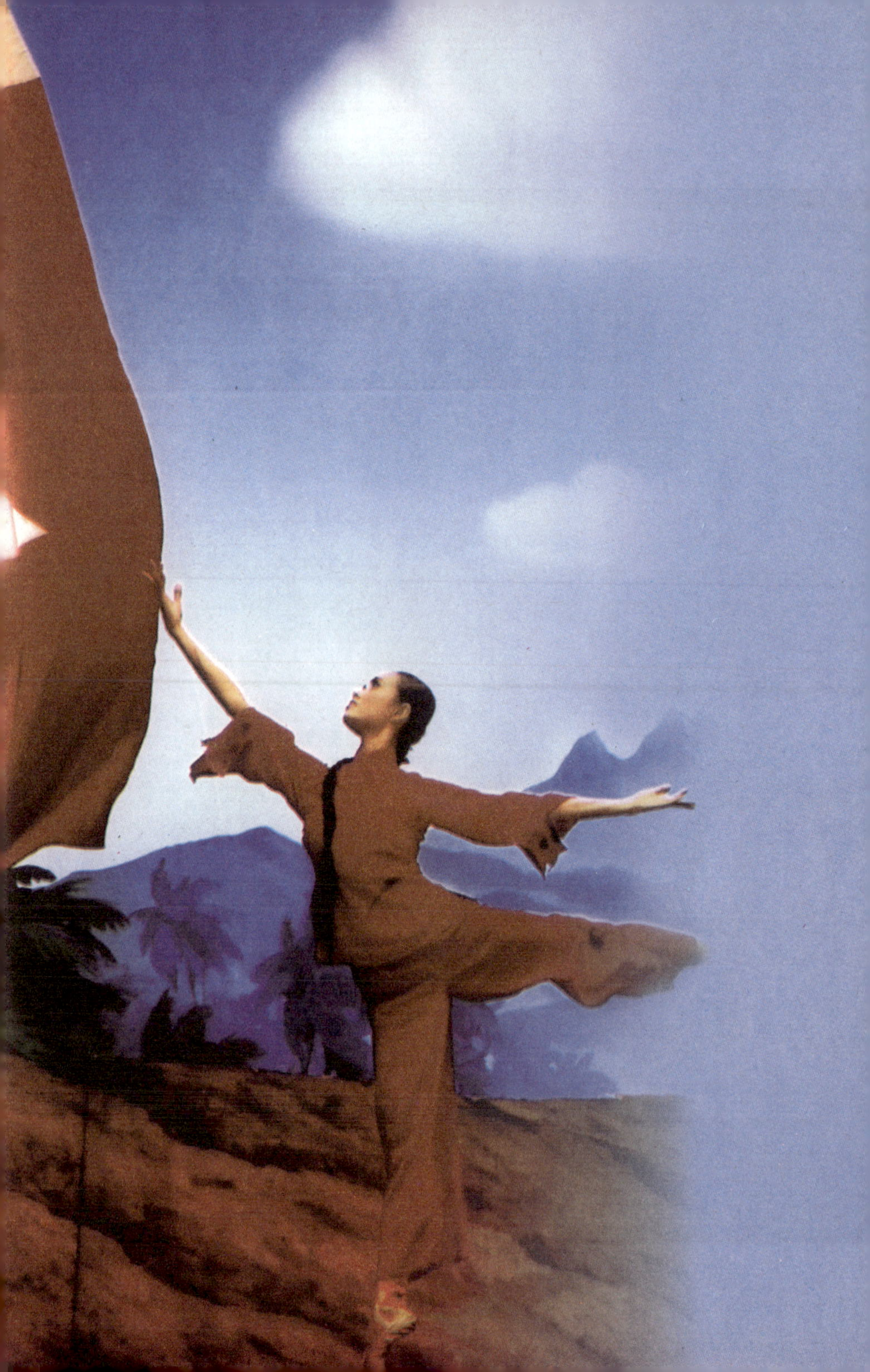

fense of the legitimate rights and interests of creators and investors, in pursuit of the country's fundamental interests. If a country fails to protect intellectual property rights, then that country's creativity will take a severe blow, and the motive force for its development will be greatly weakened. Therefore, in protecting intellectual property rights, the Chinese government's attitude is serious, earnest and resolute. We have adopted measures to continuously intensify efforts in protecting intellectual property rights: One, perfecting laws, punishing piracy according to law; two, strengthening education on the protection of intellectual property rights, calling upon the public to consciously boycott pirated goods; three, concentrating strength to control those regions and industries where the piracy phenomenon is serious; four, studying systems and mechanisms that can help solve problems for the long-term. In recent years, besides persistently strengthening daily management and law enforcement, we also carry out massive legal publicity activities. The slogan "bring pirates to court and into prison" has become widely known in society. The highest penalty that Chinese criminal law metes out for this crime is seven years imprisonment — the severest anywhere in the world. China's protection of intellectual property rights and its measures and achievements in attacking piracy have met with high praise from the inter-

■ China's modern ballets *The Red Detachment of Women* and *Raise the Red Lantern* have toured in Europe many times, winning approval in the birthplace of ballet.

national community; the Motion Picture Association of America, Time Warner and other companies specially wrote to the Chinese Ministry of Culture, fully endorsing the Chinese government's efforts and achievements in tackling piracy and protecting intellectual property rights.

■ The multimedia theatrical spectacular *ERA-Intersection of Time* combining Chinese and Western styles

VII.

The Chinese cultural market is one with tremendous potential.

The Chinese cultural market is one with tremendous potential — a boundless business opportunity, one might say. The opening-up to the outside world of China's cultural market is diversified but at the same time selective. Only fine cultural products which observe China's laws and regulations, which suit China's national conditions and popular, which benefit public's physical and mental health and facilitate social progress may have competitiveness on the Chinese market.

The gradual establishment of the socialist market economy has brought about changes in the mode of China's cultural construction. Increasingly, the market is playing a fundamental role in the allocation of resources in various fields of the national economy and social undertakings; it has greatly improved the quality, efficiency and speed of resource allocation, expanded the creation, production, distribution and consumption of spiritual and cultural products. Persisting with planned economy thinking and methods in the management and operation of culture, and for everything to come under government remit would act as a barrier to cultural development. Recognizing this, the Chinese government has clearly set the train of thought, whereby it grasps public welfare-oriented cultural work with one hand, and commercial culture business in the other hand, thus creating ever-wider scope for cultural development.

Under market economy conditions, public welfare-oriented cultural undertaking and commercial culture business resemble two wheels on a cart or two wings of a bird; neither can be overemphasized at the expense of the other. We must use market means to energetically develop cultural industry, accelerate construction of a cultural market system, perfect cultural industry policy and enhance the overall strength and competitiveness of China's cultural industry. On the other hand, this does not mean that government should give up or lighten its responsibility to provide public cultural services. Instead, it should energetically develop public welfare-oriented cultural undertaking, proceed from its duties of protecting people's basic right to share equally in cultural fruits and of improving the ideological, moral, scientific and cultural qualities of the whole people. Based on the management pattern and actual condition of the Chinese cultural undertaking at the present stage, we point to the need to gradually establish a more complete public cultural service system, one with a rational structure, balanced development, complete network, quality service and wide coverage of all society; to initially form a cultural industry pattern that takes public ownership as the mainstay whilst allowing the common development of other forms of ownership, and a cultural market pattern that takes national culture as the main body and absorbs useful cultures from outside.

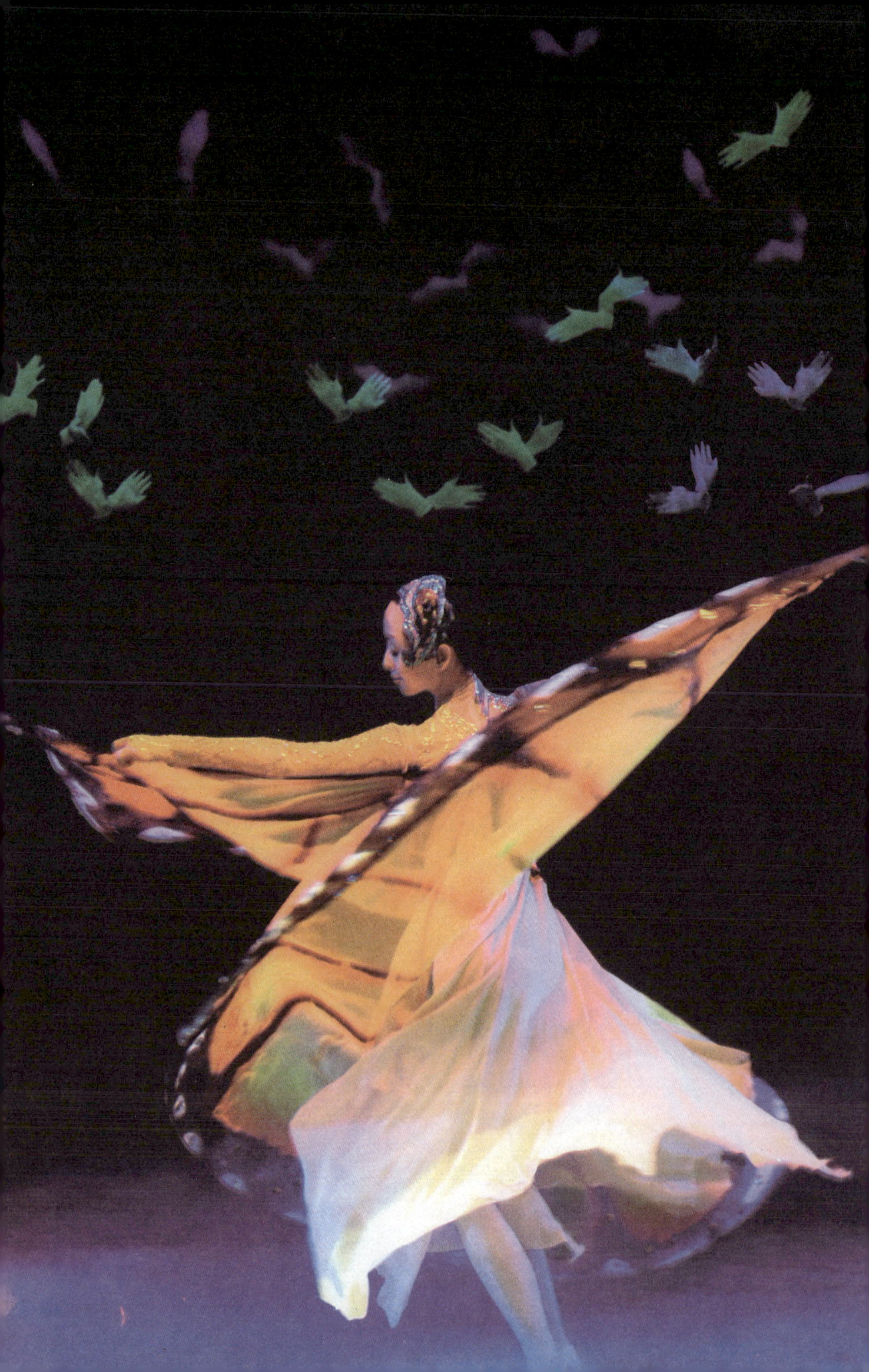

Through firm adherence to a policy of equal emphasis on the flourishing and management of art, the Chinese cultural market system has become stronger all the time. By persisting in the evenhanded approach — flourishing in one hand and management in the other hand — we have drawn up the outline for the development of the cultural market, and clearly defined the guiding idea and policy measures for the work of various markets, thus forming an orderly and favorable working structure; we have made timely adjustment to market access policy, attracted extensive private, individual and foreign investment to participate in cultural market construction, and actively cultivated mainstays of a diversified cultural market; the general framework of a cultural market system has been established in the main; great impetus has been given to changing and upgrading the business situation of the cultural market by promoting the integration of cultural industry with high and new technology, by developing modern business methods such as chain, supermarket and electronic commerce and by holding special exhibitions; the cultivation of cultural markets in rural areas and at the grass-roots level has started on the right track, and new progress has been made in the cultural work of serving farmers and grass-roots units; we have promoted the publication of relevant regulations and issued timely revisions and

Concert by Yanni at the Forbidden City

Culture is like water

as a result, cultural market policies and regulations have been gradually perfected and our ability to exercise administration according to law has been steadily improved. While carrying out the work of rectifying and standardizing the cultural market in a penetrative and persistent way and resolutely cracking down on illegal business conduct, we always keep our sights on the establishment of a mechanism for long-efficient supervision and management of the cultural market, resulting in the gradual improvement in market orderliness.

China has a long history and rich and colorful cultural resources, and against the background of deepening reforms to the cultural system and the development and perfecting of China's cultural market, there has emerged a group of exhibition institutions and performing groups with fairly good social and economic efficiencies which have established a network of their own and formed a basic framework of market for foreign performance and exhibition. However, China's cultural industry still lags behind that of developed countries. The first data released recently by the State Statistics Bureau indicate that the development of China's cultural industry has begun to take shape. But China's cultural industry's contribution to and influence on the national economy are far lower than that of developed countries; for example, the proportion of employees in the cultural industry to the total number of employees nationally is 4.77 percent in the United Sates; 7.7 percent in Britain, and 3.9 percent in Canada; the ratio of added value to the country's GDP is 5.83 percent in the United States, 7.61 percent in Britain, and 3.8 percent in Canada; the ratio of these two indices stays at about 1:1, as compared with China's 1.8:1, showing that the value-creating ability of China's cultural industry is still relatively low. Regional imbalance in the Chinese cultural industry development is conspicuous. The scale of cultural industrial development and income-earning ability of the economically developed provinces of eastern China are both much greater than in central and western China; the regional disparity of cultural industrial development is greater than the regional disparity in GDP. We will persist in taking the government as the leading factor, folk exchange as the mainstay and market mechanism as the lever to give full play to initiatives by central and local governments; combine governmental exchange with people-to-people exchange, and cultural diplomacy with cultural trade. We will continue to strengthen the systems and mechanisms of foreign cultural trade, and give play to the government's role as regulator and driving force. We will speed up the establishment of a statuary system for foreign cultural trade, so as to create for enterprises a favorable legal environment for foreign cultural trade. We will improve supplementary policies for foreign cultural trade and create necessary conditions expanding the international market for cultural enterprises in the aspects of banking, insurance, foreign exchange, finance and taxation, talent, law, information service, entry and exit management. We will establish a foreign cultural trade statistic index and data study system, as a service for the formulation of government policy and enterprise decisions.

Since accession to the WTO in 2001, China has further intensified its efforts to open to the outside world. Alongside China's continuously strengthened protection of intellectual property rights, bigger efforts have also been made in regards to accessibility of the Chinese cultural market. The range of accessibility is now very wide. Furthermore, it should be pointed out that China is relaxing controls over the range of cultural market access in a context where the market economy system is not long established, where the cultural industry has not yet grown to a large scale and where the market mechanism is not yet perfect; as a consequence, we face both opportunities and severe challenges.

The American production of musical *Cats* staged in Beijing

However, we are full of confidence. We will unwaveringly persist in opening to the outside world and strive to improve the quality of national cultural products and their international market competitiveness by implementing the strategy for excellent national cultural products. We will continue to deepen reform of the cultural system and enhance the self-development vigor of national culture. The Chinese cultural market is one with tremendous potential — a boundless business opportunity, one might say. The opening of the Chinese cultural market to the outside world is diversified and at the same time selective. Only excellent cultural products, that are in observance of China's laws and regulations and in conformity with China's national condition and people's will, that benefit people's physical and mental health and facilitate social progress, may have competitiveness on the Chinese market. We welcome entrepreneurs of various countries to come to invest in the Chinese cultural market in accordance with agreements already reached. We will keep our promises to provide them with conveniences as far as possible.

Along with the deepening trend towards economic globalization, cultural trade has become an important element of international trade. According to UNESCO figures, the total volume of global cultural trade jumped from US$95.3 billion in 1980 to U$387.9 billion in 1998. However, the bulk of the trade was carried out among a few developed countries. In 1990, the cultural export trade of Japan, the United States, Germany and Britain represented 55.4 per-

CULTURE IS LIKE WATER

cent of the volume of global cultural export trade in that year, while the cultural import trade volume was highly concentrated in the United States, Germany, Britain and France, representing 47 percent of global cultural import trade volume in that year. After 2000, adjustments were made in the ranking of

A choir from Yunnan Province gave performances of original music during the Chinese Cultural Festival held in the US.

large countries in terms of cultural import and export trade, but there was no change in the general pattern. In 2004, China, with a total trade volume of U$1.15 trillion, became one of the world's three biggest trade powers. As China became an international trade power, its foreign cultural trade also grew by a big margin. But, taken as a whole, compared with the overall growth rate of China's foreign trade, cultural trade still lags far behind and there exists an enormous trade deficit; China's culture-related exports in particular still are a very weak link.

Both exchange and openness are equal and mutually beneficial. In the interest of national prosperity and progress, of world peace and development, China's attitude toward opening to the outside world is sincere and resolute. China needs to understand the world; every day its media is informing the Chinese people about world development and change, including huge amounts of information from the United States and other developed countries regarding scientific and technological inventions and economic development. However, some people in the United States and other Western countries are concerned about China's openness and seem to be entering the Chinese market only in a one-sided way. Some Western media seldom make objective reports on the situation in China. This is very unfavorable to opening-up and exchange. Over the past two decades, China's enthusiasm for getting to know the culture and current situation of the United States and the world at large seems to way exceed that of the other side. I am struck by this every time I visit the United States. Many American friends think this needs thinking about and paying attention to. What I feel pleased about is that there has been some change in this situation, there are still aspects that are not as one would wish. Last year, the occasion when I was delivering a speech in the United States was precisely the moment when a new round of disputes on China-US trade issues was on the rise. I expressed my views frankly to my American friends. China-US relations are not all plain sailing; conflicts, friction, disputes and differences are all to be expected. What is crucial is how to understand and handle them. Here I want to take up the matter of China-US trade. I am neither a foreign minister, nor a commerce minister, I just want to say something about my personal perspective as culture minister. There is intense dispute over the China-US trade problem. Our two countries' trade departments have engaged in many rounds of negotiations and have achieved quite good results recently. In terms of trade in material goods, the United States invariably stresses its huge trade deficit; however, in terms of trade in cultural products, China's trade deficit is even bigger. Here I have several figures: Between 2000 and 2004, China imported 4,332 films through various channels, of which American films accounted for 40-50 percent; of the more than 4,000 foreign films broadcast by Chinese Central Television and local television stations, over 40 percent were American films; of the 211 imported films shown in cinemas, 53 percent were American; of the 88 films imported by the separate account method during the five years, 70 were American films, accounting for 80 percent of the total. Can anyone present here answer these questions: How many Chinese films are now broadcast and shown in the United States? How many Chinese cultural products are there in the American market? It can be said that there are very few! It is abnormal that China's cultural trade with the United States should show such a large deficit but we do not blame the Americans too much, rather, we take a greater look at our own part in this. China's cultural products are not bad, and American audiences welcome them, but we lack a marketing network and marketing experience; not fully understanding marketing methods, we need to study harder, at the same time we hope the United States will further open its market, so that more good Chinese cultural products will enter the United States.

With regard to the problem of their trade deficit, I think American friends need to have a calm mind and development vision. If only the United States changes its discriminatory policy of trade with China it can increase its exports to China, and with increased exports its trade deficit will naturally be reduced. The practice of imposing various kinds of prohibitions on exports to China and setting up various types of restriction on commodities from China is disadvantageous to the development of China-US trade. To be quite frank, China began to understand the market economy and the WTO quite late in the day and America is China's teacher in this regard. But why did this set of rules taught by the teacher not apply when we used them for dealings with the United States? The Chinese market is so vast, given America's economic strength and high scientific and technological level, it is entirely possible to achieve the aim of increasing exports to China and reducing its trade deficit with China. At present, the cost of an American Boeing plane is equivalent to the cost of lots of Chinese garments, shoes, hats and dolls. Accordingly, it is said that one should not take a short-sighted approach toward China-US trade issues, but rather take a long-term view; one should not just look at the simple figures, but should have a calm mind and work to a single standard. From a long-term perspective, I think America has the advantage whether in terms of strength or of actual benefit.

The Chinese always like to "meet friends through writings" and this more or less reflects the nature of culture. Culture originally came into being to meet a communication need. Culture originates from the mind and reaches directly to the mind. Culture is like water, flowing and surging, passing through mountains and ridges and emptying into the sea from all directions. Culture flows and shines, linking different countries and peoples and the hearts of people of different cultures, makes the earth, this common homeland of humanity, more colorful and graceful; culture brings to mankind a brighter light in his longing for the future...

图书在版编目（CIP）数据

文化如水 / 孙家正著；梁发明译. －北京：外文出版社，2006
（中国的和平发展系列）
ISBN 7-119-04494-X

I.文... II.①孙...②梁... III.文化事业 - 概况 - 中国 - 英文
IV.G12

中国版本图书馆 CIP 数据核字（2006）第 069205 号

作　　者	孙家正
责任编辑	崔黎丽
助理编辑	薛芊
英文翻译	梁发明
英文审定	Paul White　王明杰
内文及封面设计	天下智慧文化传播公司
执行设计	姚　波
制　　作	外文出版社照排中心
印刷监制	冯　浩

文化如水

*

© 外文出版社

外文出版社出版
（中国北京百万庄大街 24 号）
邮政编码 100037
北京外文印刷厂印刷
中国国际图书贸易总公司发行
（中国北京车公庄西路 35 号）
北京邮政信箱第 399 号　邮政编码 100044
2006 年(大 32 开)第 1 版
2006 年 12 月第 1 版　第 1 次印刷
（英）
ISBN 7-119-04494-X
17-E-3738P